METAMORPHOSIS

An Odyssey of the Spirit

by

John Mulkey

Metamorphosis

Published and Distributed by:
Rebel Publishing
PO Box 90037
Sioux Falls, SD 57109
U.S.A.

First Printing April 2002

John Mulkey

Acknowledgments

I would like to thank my wife, Francisca, without whose encouragement, love, and patience, this book might never have been completed. I extend special thanks to my publisher, Michael Cox, for his enthusiasm and for giving me an opportunity to share some of my experiences. I also thank all my loving friends who helped me improve some truly rough drafts.

Finally, and in true appreciation of his efforts, I thank John Perkins for his tireless work toward preserving the Amazon rain forest and the amazing wisdom of its remarkable people. My brief time with his friends in the jungle changed my life in ways I'm only beginning to appreciate. I recommend John's non-profit organization, Dream Change Coalition, to all who struggle to understand and protect our wondrous planet.

Dedication

This book is dedicated to Lindsay, an angel whose light, though much too brief, continues to brighten my path.

Table of Contents

CHAPTER 1

WINDS OF CHANGE

A sudden gust caught the crest of a swell, stinging my face and resurrecting me from my stupor. The wind was picking up. The icy spray dripped into my eyes and I wiped it away, then eased my tongue across my lips. They tasted of salt and dried blood. I scanned the horizon, searching for something to focus upon—trees, land, a boat, something—anything. Nothing. Nothing penetrated the wall of gray that had imprisoned me for three days. Fog. Thick, damnable fog. The cold tentacles of mist pried at my jacket and I tugged on the zipper, pulling it to my neck.

A vision of impending news reports flashed across my mind. "Local writer vanishes in freak spring storm."

No, I wasn't published enough to be recognized as a writer, but then, I was too far removed from my old profession for them to be aware of what I'd once done. "Local man vanishes." I smiled, contemplating the fantasied reporter's dilemma. Perhaps my disappearance wouldn't be newsworthy.

The storm had blown out of nowhere and was gone six hours later. That's probably all that saved me; a couple more hours of wind would have put me on the bottom for sure. When I left port the weather didn't look great, but I thought a little rough water might be fun. I hadn't expected a gale.

I stepped into the cockpit and gripped the wheel. I was probably miles from the shipping lanes. Not much chance of being discovered. They wouldn't look south. They'd search north, towards Portland, where I told Charlie I was going, before I changed my mind.

The trip began on Wednesday, March 6, when I sailed out of Wareham, heading for Portland, Maine. I'd wanted to get away for months, to separate myself from my depressing surroundings, and had no idea when I'd return. Shortly after sailing, though, I had an urge to turn south, towards Nantucket. Relaxing for a couple of days would be a great start to my trip, I thought, and the island's windswept moors might help erase the difficult past from memory.

My decision to take the boat out had been a bad idea. She was unprepared and so was I. Though she wasn't necessarily old, too much time had passed without experiencing the open sea. *Conquest,* a name given during her racing years, was a thirty-one foot, Atkin sloop of cedar and oak, built in Boothbay, Maine.

Once sleek and proud, in earlier times she'd been a real beauty. But years of inattention had left her tired and dispirited, and she'd languished at her slip, gathering barnacles. The lady had lost her panache. I was foolish to risk her in such rough seas, crazy to take her out alone.

Conquest's condition, however, wasn't the problem. With more than half my life gone, I'd never reached an understanding of my existence, never discovered the reasons for my being. *Why was I here? What was my purpose?* My own futile search for meaning had led me to act irresponsibly, and the answers I'd sought remained as obscure as ever, impenetrable, like the fog in which I drifted.

The gray wall before me became a screen on which I projected my thoughts. A vision formed of a time, six years before, when Susan and I had sailed to Bar Harbor, probably the best time we ever spent together.

For three weeks we explored some of the most wonderful villages along the New England coast, sailing, playing, and gorging on lobster and steamed crab. It was a time of capriciousness, renewed romance—forgotten a few months after we returned. That was the year my restlessness intensified, a time begun in innocence and ending in disaster, when I lost my job, my self-confidence, and my wife.

Susan said I'd fallen into a terminal mid-life crisis, and maybe I had. However, I'd gone far beyond a turning point. I'd reached the point of no return.

I'd spent fourteen years with American Financial Resources, one of the largest investment firms in Boston, but I felt trapped, worthless. The most meaningful thing I'd done was chairing a popular local fund-raiser. That was a sterling achievement. We often spent more on our clothes and entertainment than we raised in donations, but I was praised in the society column: "Dynamo Dan does it again for the kids." The thought of it made me sick.

Leaving the corporation was a decision made on impulse, another attempt to define a life devoid of meaning. I'd planned to write a novel, seeking purpose in the fame and success I thought my writing would generate—even had the foolish confidence I could do it. I had visions of myself at Marblehead relishing the kudos that would surely follow. I'd read the self-help books, taken creative writing courses, and joined the local writer's club. Looking back, it would seem funny if the pain weren't so fresh in my mind.

Susan seemed to know I was on the wrong track and was quick to remind me of my slim chances for success. But I'd refused to listen, having set my course long before. With or without her, I planned to see it through.

Four years passed before I could admit she'd been right. I'd made a dreadful mistake, responsible for my misery and for destroying my marriage and career. My ego could no longer protect me from the truth.

If only I could be normal. Where was the peace, the happiness I perceived in others? I'd never found the answers on my own, and God wasn't listening to my questions.

****

The fog was a smothering blanket. If there were a ship out there, I'd never see it. I listened, hoping to hear the familiar, *thump, thump, thump,* of a freighter, but the only sound was *Conquest's* creaking and moaning as she wallowed through the swells.

Suddenly, a high-pitched screech pierced the morning calm. It was like the call of a bird—but not quite. The call came again, louder, closer. As I looked up, a gigantic bird swooped out of the fog, passing directly overhead.

Three times I heard the frightful shriek and three times the creature flew by me, so close I could see its feathers rippled by the wind. It didn't look like any bird I'd ever seen—it was certainly no sea bird—and was as big as an eagle.

As the beast made its third pass, its head turned towards me—tiny black eyes staring directly into mine. For a brief moment I felt a connection with my strange visitor from the mist. Then, with one final and dreadful shriek, it vanished.

I looked skyward and listened for several minutes, repulsed, yet paradoxically attracted to the thing, wondering where it had gone. It knew how to reach land. If I could follow . . .

My attention returned to the fog, and I leaned forward pressing against the rail. The air was heavy with unbearable silence. I listened, turning my head from side to side. With senses sharpened by my grim predicament, I heard another sound, not the bird, something different. A muffled thump. Another boat! Starboard, off the bow. I heard it more clearly and ran forward calling out, "Ahoy, ahoy." My words were a dull knife against the opaque vapor.

I grabbed the horn and gave a long blast, then another and another, listening for a reply. I sounded again and squeezed the trigger until the canister was empty and my fingers were numb. There was no response.

Without warning, something appeared a few yards off the bow. I could see movement. It was a boat! Jesus, a skiff, a rowboat! A lone, dark figure sat motionless in the center.

The boat banged into *Conquest,* and I leaped toward the rail. "Hey," I yelled. "What are you doing out here? In that thing? Are you lost?"

The figure turned toward me, his face obscured in the shadow of a large, floppy hat. "No. Are you?"

A chill ran through my body. Something told me to be on guard.

"I've lost my sail and my engine," I said. "Been drifting for three days. Do you know where we are?"

The stranger lashed his boat to mine and reached over to grab the rail, tossing his hat into the skiff as he climbed on deck. "Come aboard," I said, trying to show authority. "My name's Dan Murphy. Not much of a sailor, though. I was afraid I might wind up in Newfoundland. Can't believe we found each other out here. Where'd you come from?"

He ignored my question and stepped toward the cabin. "What's the trouble with the engine?" he asked.

"I don't know. When the storm hit, I lowered the sail, but I took on a little water. I think it flooded. I drained the batteries trying to get it started. After the wind subsided I tried to put the sail back up, but a wave caught it and tore it loose. It's been dragging for a couple of days, like a sea anchor."

The stranger started down the ladder. "I'll look at the engine."

"Forget it," I said. "There's not enough power in the batteries to operate the radio. That's why I couldn't call for help."

Before I could stop him, the stranger entered the cabin, lifted the hatch, and crawled into the engine compartment.

"You're wasting your time," I said. "Even if you could find the problem, you couldn't start it. There's no power."

"Hand me a screwdriver. You have one, don't you? And a flashlight."

"Sure, but I tell you it's no use." I lifted the dinette cushion and pulled out my toolbox.

"Here." I reached into the hatch.

"Make some coffee. I like it strong."

Startled by his gruff command, I backed away. "Okay."

I lit the burner and poured water into the coffee pot. Scraping and bumping sounds came from the bilge. As the water steamed to a boil, the engine gave a reluctant grumble and began a rhythmic coughing and sputtering.

I leaned into the hatch. "What's going on?" I said.

A loud roar from the open compartment startled me, and I stumbled backward, falling across the open toolbox. I yelled out in pain as the engine sprang to life.

"What'd you do?" I shouted.

The stranger ignored my question and crawled out of the bilge, turning to face me, his craggy features amplified by a disapproving scowl. I guessed him to be in his sixties, although he appeared unusually fit. Stooping in the limited headroom of the cabin, he stared at me for several seconds from dark, deep set eyes.

"How did you do that?" I demanded. "The batteries are dead. It's impossible"

"Yes, impossible," he responded. He gave a brief smile. "Your generator needs attention too." He turned and climbed to the deck.

7

I hesitated briefly, then followed up the ladder, filled with questions. "How did you get out here? In that thing." I pointed towards the skiff.

His boat appeared to be very old, but in perfect shape. Too perfect. It was freshly painted, clean, no scuffmarks. It belonged in a museum. Its most striking feature, however, was that it had no sail and, more incredibly, no oars. I stared in disbelief.

"I don't understand how you got here," I said. "We're miles from shore. Did you come from another boat?"

"What about the coffee?" he asked.

"Uh . . . of course, I'll get you a cup."

I clambered down the ladder and fumbled through the galley, searching for a clean cup. Muffled sounds came from above. I paused and listened. Silence. I poured the coffee and called out, "It's ready." There was no reply. I called again.

I climbed to the deck. It was deserted. Both the stranger and his boat were gone. I walked to the rail where it had been tied. The line that had secured the skiff to *Conquest* was neatly coiled on deck, as it had been before the stranger appeared. There was no indication he'd ever been there.

What had happened? Was I hallucinating? I staggered toward the cockpit, the stranger's coffee still in hand. As I collapsed onto the cushion, I pressed the cup to my lips. The steaming liquid scalded my tongue, and I leaned over the rail, emptying it into the cold Atlantic. I needed something stronger. I reached into the locker and pulled out a bottle of Scotch, filled my cup and drank slow and long. The Scotch burned too, but in a good way, and I savored the taste and warm sensation it created flowing into my stomach.

An hour later, the bottle was empty, and I'd convinced myself the experience was merely a strange and powerful delusion caused by my lack of sleep. My rationalizing was halted, though, as I became aware of the engine idling below. It had obviously been running since the stranger disappeared, and sounded better than it had in years. How could I have been unaware of the sound, the vibration? Something had happened, something powerful and bizarre.

Regardless of the cause, the engine was running. I had to get under way. I went below and searched for something to cut away the remains of the tattered sail. As I grabbed a knife, my eyes were drawn to the dinette. There, in the middle of the table was a bunch of papers held together with a rusty safety pin, an article torn from a magazine. The title was circled with a red marker: *Psychic Healing—Myth or Miracle?*

My hands gripped the pages as questions raced through my mind. Where had they come from? I'd never seen them before, and they couldn't have been there earlier. Perhaps the stranger had dropped them. There was comfort in knowing I had confirmation of the stranger's appearance. I tossed the pages onto the table and climbed on deck.

The air was lighter with a slight breeze blowing from the south. I cut away the sail, watched it drift away, then settled into the cockpit. I sat there for several minutes before pushing the throttle forward. The smooth, steady sound of the engine was encouraging, and I congratulated myself for having added an extra fuel tank several years earlier. I didn't know where I was, but I felt I'd be okay.

Then, it hit me. I had power! The batteries were charging. The GPS was working! I could check my location and chart a course for home.

The Global Positioning System must have been invented for sailors like me. With only marginal navigational skills, I was totally dependent upon the GPS, but it more than made up for my shortcomings. Through the wonders of satellite technology, it could show my location with amazing accuracy. I went into the cabin, turned it on, and began charting a new course, surprised at how little I'd drifted. I was less than twenty miles from the coast.

Once back at the wheel, I steered through the dissipating fog. I took a deep breath, bathing my lungs in the damp morning air. Though I'd had little sleep, I was unusually alert.

In little more than an hour the fog was gone and patches of clear blue sky appeared overhead. I estimated my speed to be about six knots. At that rate, I'd reach a place to anchor before dark. I could refuel and be home the next day.

Three hours passed uneventfully, and, as the fourth hour approached, the outline of land appeared. I'd made it. If my navigating was correct, I was approaching Monomoy Island. I could anchor near Hyannis, have a decent meal, and get the first full night of sleep in three days.

With my ordeal ending, my thoughts returned to the problems I'd faced before leaving, the very reasons I'd taken the trip. Getting away had been a diversion, a voyage to help me forget the predicament I'd created for myself. As usual, nothing had gone right. I cursed my luck, wondering what would be next.

CHAPTER 2

A NEW COURSE

Two months had passed since returning from my misadventure, and I'd pushed the bizarre parts from my mind, convinced that a static surge had caused the engine to start. Sure it was strange, but I didn't try to analyze what had happened. There were more pressing problems at hand.

Unable to find inspiration and lacking the discipline to force myself into a routine, I struggled with my writing, continually searching for distractions. My cruising fiasco—and several concerned friends—had convinced me to forget Portland, at least until *Conquest* and I were better prepared. But my narrow escape did prove to be of some benefit. I'd gained a firsthand view of the deplorable condition the boat had fallen into, and I began to spend a lot of physical effort, but little money, attempting to restore her to a more seaworthy state.

She needed more than cosmetic work, though. There was serious maintenance to do, far beyond my limited knowledge; but I did what I knew: cleaning, scraping, painting.

****

The entire afternoon had been spent struggling with the generator, and I'd discovered the limits of both my patience and abilities. I reached over and gave the switch a quick turn. The thing refused to start. I turned it again, harder the second time. Still no response. I kept trying until the battery was drained. Dammit, after eighteen years of service, the Onan had finally died. I threw a pair of rusty pliers against the mute mass of iron. Three hours of squatting in the bilge, amid the stench of diesel fuel and rotting timbers, was more than I could bear. I crawled over to the hatch, pulled myself onto the cabin floor and lay there for several minutes, working the cramps from my back and legs.

I shouldn't have been surprised. The generator had been overheating for weeks and had become increasingly difficult to start. When the mechanic had last worked on it, he'd said it wasn't worth overhauling. But it couldn't have failed at a worse time. My end of the dock didn't have shore power, and I needed the generator to keep the batteries charged for the lights and the laptop. I sighed and slid onto the dinette. Hell, there was no use worrying about it. The damn thing had quit and I couldn't fix it.

It was almost 6:00 P.M. The day had been a total waste. I'd changed the oil, replaced the fuel filter, and cleaned and tightened everything else, hoping it might make a difference, but it hadn't. I stumbled towards the icebox—my legs didn't want to work—and pulled out a soda. No, that wasn't what I needed. I was more than thirsty. I slipped my hand around my best friend, a half-empty bottle of Scotch. I grabbed a cup and climbed the ladder to the deck.

A strong breeze from the west felt cool against my damp shirt, and I settled into the cockpit, gently placing the Scotch beside me. The marina was quiet, even for a Wednesday. I liked that. Most of the neighboring boats were owned by weekend sailors and there was never much going on through the week. The solitude was what had attracted me to the place in the beginning; that, and the price.

Three boats down from me, Charlie, the dock boy, was scrubbing down "*Figaro.*" He glanced up as I came on deck.

"Get it fixed?" he called.

"No. This time I think it's beyond help."

"Whatcha gonna do for power?" Charlie stopped scrubbing and shuffled up the ramp. "I've got enough wire to reach you. I can run it over. 'Course, you'll have to unhook if anybody comes around."

"No thanks, Charlie. I'll do something. Wouldn't want to get you in trouble."

"I don't care. Mr. Peterson don't come down here 'cept on weekends and the first of the month. Anyhow, he likes you. He won't care if you use a little."

"No, Charlie. I still haven't . . ." I paused, deciding not to say I hadn't paid the previous month's slip rental. "I don't want to take any of his power. It's okay. Don't worry about it."

13

Charlie returned to his scrubbing. "Just wanted to help. Let me know if you need to plug in to re-charge or something. I'll do it for you. Want me to ask Bert to look at the Onan?"

"No thanks. He's already passed judgment on it. I don't think he can revive it now, unless he knows some magic. Anyway, Dr. Gordon has been after me to sell him the dinghy, and he just bought a new eight-kilowatt Westerbeke. Maybe I can trade for his old generator. It probably has a few good years left in it."

I re-filled my cup and leaned back against the frayed cushion. The boat's gentle rocking was hypnotic. I looked to the west where trees effused the last rays of sun, a shimmering glow that danced across the ripples of the bay. The play of light and shadow created a kaleidoscope of patterns on the boats around me, and I tried to translate the scene into a poem. The words wouldn't come. Sights and sounds that once impassioned my senses failed to provide inspiration, and my pen remained idle. I tossed my notebook through the open cabin door, poured the last of the Scotch, and drank slowly.

The sun had gone, leaving its golden reflection on a thin layer of clouds. The setting was beautiful, but meaningless, and I was angered by my inability to describe it.

Perhaps I should forget writing, I thought, go to Boston and get my old job back. Maybe I could start over. But how would I do it? I had no idea. Any decision could wait until tomorrow. I was exhausted. I climbed down the ladder, collapsed onto the bunk, and immediately fell asleep.

The rhythmic clanking of a dozen mast cables woke me and I peered out into the gray morning light. A brisk wind was churning the bay. The weather report had predicted thunderstorms. It might be a good idea to spend a day or two in town.

I slid off the bunk, pulled on a sweatshirt, and plodded into the head. Standing before the mirror, I examined the face staring back at me. I hated it. It wasn't mine. It was my father's. In recent years I'd grown to look just like him—the same ruddy complexion, pale thin lips, and a forehead continually growing larger.

I leaned forward, inspecting the face more closely. When had the wrinkles around the eyes grown larger, deeper? When had the skin become dull and lifeless? The image in the mirror was unwelcome, an old man taking shelter in my body.

I went into the galley and lit the stove. As I placed the pot on the open flame, I shook the coffee can. Empty. A search of the locker revealed nothing more than a jar of instant, hardened into an unrecognizable mass of brown sludge. I scraped some into my cup, poured in the water, and climbed to the deck. Dark clouds were building in the south.

How could I start over? I was forty-nine years old. No one would want an old, has-been, especially one who'd already checked out on the establishment. How could I make the right connection and find someone who would give me a chance? The problem was, I didn't want another job. Thoughts of the corporate scene nauseated me.

Like it or not, though, I had to have some money soon. A job seemed the only logical way.

I decided to call Ted Linder from my old days in corporate life. He'd worked for me at AFR and over the years we developed a pretty good friendship. Though he'd called me several times after I left the company, I'd always found reasons to be unavailable. The last couple of times I found his messages on the recorder, I couldn't bring myself to return the call. I suppose I was embarrassed about my lack of meaningful work, but Ted had said to call if I needed anything. Well, I needed something. I wouldn't want

15

him to think I was looking for a job though. I'd say I was bored and looking for a new challenge.

My hands fumbled through a pile of papers on the chart table. Though it had only been four years since I'd left the company, I couldn't remember the phone number, and searched for several minutes before locating it under a stack of past-due bills. The slick white business card, still crisp and impressive, glistened in the morning light.

"Most expensive card stock available," the printer had said. I walked to the window and read the copy: Daniel R. Murphy, Executive Vice President. Jesus, that seemed a lifetime ago.

I held the card for several minutes as pictures from the past flashed through my mind. There had been a few good times, when life was more ordered and I'd been in control. I swallowed hard against the lump that formed in my throat. I missed the legitimacy my old life had provided.

The year prior to leaving the company, however, had shaped a different perspective. I'd grown jaded to the success, indifferent to the business, and compelled to try something new. Jack, my boss, had suggested I take a sabbatical. His vision of my problem was that I was tired, in need of a temporary change of scenery. He had more difficulty than anyone understanding how I could leave forever.

Leaving forever, though, was certainly my intention, but I'd begun to question more than my leaving. I questioned my reason for existing. Life had become a labyrinth of discouraging events, and every turn served to amplify my confusion. Maybe Ted could give some idea, some connection to help me get a fresh start. Although a job wasn't what I wanted, having an income was critical. It was worth a try. I picked up the phone and dialed.

"Mr. Linder's office, may I help you?" The soft voice on the other end stirred my memory. My god, it was Kay! I couldn't believe she was still there.

Kay had been my assistant for more than five years and had worked with me on some of my most difficult projects. She was an employer's dream, bright, fiercely dedicated, with the uncanny ability of anticipating every request. She had no family, which made it easier for me to ask her to work nights and weekends, and as far as I knew, had no serious relationships. Her attitude and commitment had made my job much easier. Other than Susan, she was the best friend I ever had. On more than one occasion, Susan had accused me of having an affair with Kay. Though that never happened, there were times I wished it had.

Once when we'd worked until midnight, Kay looked at me, her deep blue eyes sparkling, and said, "You're probably the only man I ever really cared for, but more importantly for me, you're my best friend. I'd never want to do anything to jeopardize our friendship."

I made some inane remark about the importance of friendship, but inwardly, I was embarrassed, knowing she'd read my thoughts. She was a good friend, and as my relationship with Susan deteriorated, I occasionally had thoughts beyond that.

Kay was attractive—tall, slender, with a smile for everyone—but there was some unidentifiable something that kept me from ever approaching her on a sexual level. It was more than wanting to remain faithful to Susan. Hell, by the time I left the company, my relationship with Susan was already headed for disaster, and I'm not sure she cared what I did, as long as I paid the bills and didn't embarrass her.

"May I help you," the voice on the other end asked a second time. I coughed and slipped my hand over the mouthpiece, "Ted Linder," I said, muffling my voice. For reasons unknown even to me, I didn't want her to know I was on the line. "Just a moment please, I'll connect you."

"Ted Linder," spoke the familiar voice on the other end of the line.

"Ted, this is Dan—Dan Murphy, how are you?"

Ted paused before answering. "Dan? Well, this is certainly a surprise. How's my old buddy doing?"

"Oh, I'm fine. I'm coming up to Boston tomorrow and thought maybe we could have lunch or something. Are you free?"

"I'm not free, but I'm pretty cheap," Ted responded and laughed. "Sure, I'd love to see you, but I have an appointment for lunch. How about meeting me after work, at Riordan's? We can have a beer and a bowl of clam chowder, just like the old days."

"Great," I responded. "What time?"

"How about six-thirty? Wish I could chat, but I'm late for a meeting with Jack. Gotta go. See you tomorrow."

****

I awoke the next morning, anxious about my meeting with Ted and left for Boston soon after lunch. Traffic was unusually light and I arrived earlier than expected. I drove around trying to develop a strategy. I didn't want Ted to know the truth.

It had been several months since I'd been in town and I revisited some of my favorite districts, recalling the vitality and youthfulness Boston exhibited. Although the place seems a bit provincial at times, that's part of the charm, the attraction it holds. Boston isn't New York and doesn't want to be.

After a quick tour I headed to Riordan's to have a drink before Ted arrived. I hoped a little Scotch might stimulate the brain cells and help me with him.

Riordan's looked exactly as it had when I'd last seen it about four years before. It had the same dark paneling, worn brass rail, and ancient fans overhead. Nothing had changed. Of course, not much had changed since it had first opened, which I'd been told, was around eighteen-hundred.

Indulging myself, I ordered a double Chivas and began to stare into my glass as if it were a crystal ball. I watched small cracks develop in the ice and fill with the golden brown of my magic elixir. Scotch, a perfume to cover the stench of life. A couple of years before, two or three drinks a week were the norm; but it had begun to take four or five just to remove the pain of one night.

Down at the end of the bar, a guy in a wrinkled suit was desperately trying every line he knew on a girl probably half his age. I'd seen the type, on the road most of the year with a wife and three kids at home. He was drooling over a girl that wouldn't normally get much attention. The scene was comical, right out of a cheap movie and he wasn't having any luck. The line he needs to use, I thought, the only one that will get the response he wants, is: "How much?"

I returned my attention to the glass, hypnotized by the swirling blend of ice and alcohol. Raising it to my lips, I took a quick gulp, then another, and was ready to order a second when I heard someone calling my name. "Dan, is that you? My god, you look. . . uh . . . different. I almost didn't recognize you, especially with the beard."

Ted grabbed my hand as I spun around, maintaining a tight grip as he spoke. "Looks like you've added a little more gray too" he said. "How have you been? Damn, it's good to see you. Things just haven't been the same since you left. I have to think for myself now." His face widened into a broad grin.

He was likable, with a jovial attitude that always put me at ease. I'd recruited him from a competitor who failed to recognize his potential. With only a little mentoring, Ted became one of our best account managers ever. He was a great student and thrived on the stress and chaos that were inherent parts of the business. In many ways, I suppose, he reminded me of myself when I began my career. His attitude and intensity had even caused me to regain some of my interest, at least for a time. And like most of us, he'd become intoxicated by the money and the fast-paced opportunities that brought so much success during the nineties.

"Sorry," he said, "I can't stay long. I promised Beth I'd be home by seven-thirty. She has a club meeting or something."

Ted grabbed a stool, sat down and leaned forward. "What happened, Dan?" he said. He furrowed his brow. "Christ, you just disappeared. You said you'd stay in touch."

There were reasons I hadn't stayed in touch, but I didn't want to explain. I didn't want to discuss the failures or the few successes, which had been mostly insignificant. I'd sold nothing of consequence in almost a year. No one would understand what had happened, how I could reach such a low state, so quickly after being on top.

Perhaps it had been guilt that led me to give everything to Susan, the house, the furniture, the money. I wanted nothing except the beach house, confident I would recover quickly. I'd traded the world of business for the literary world, blindly anticipating instant success and oblivious to the absurdity of my actions. My decision had been a grievous mistake. I had no intention of discussing what had happened. I wanted to forget that part of my life.

"I honestly thought you'd come back," Ted said. "I guess you were serious when you told us you'd had enough." He shook his head. "What's it like being a writer?"

"It's pretty boring," I said. I wanted to change the subject. "What's going on at the company?"

My strategy worked. Ted gave me a quick update on what had happened since I'd left. Almost everything had changed. AFR's client list and revenues had nearly doubled. Ted had been promoted and handled most of my old accounts. I grimaced, realizing how well things were moving without me and wondered if I could ever fit in. Would I be able to survive what had become an unfamiliar environment.

"Dan, you remember Dr. West, don't you? Mike West?" Ted's voice jerked me back to the present. "You know, the surgeon, the big account I landed just before you left. In the last couple of years he's withdrawn almost two-thirds of his cash, and from the looks of things, his account could be empty within a year or so.

"He's crazy," Ted said. He seemed to think I cared. I didn't. Oblivious to my lack of interest, he continued. "The guy's been traveling for almost three years, but it's no vacation. He's on a mission or something. He calls me every few months and has me transfer funds to whatever city he finds himself in."

I interrupted and called the bartender over. "Refill here and one for my friend."

"Just a light beer for me, thanks." Ted paused while we waited for our drinks.

When the glasses arrived he raised his toward me. "To good friends," he said. He took a sip and continued his story. "It didn't seem strange at first. Doctor West would call from Phoenix, San Francisco, or

21

other normal places, but then the calls started coming from weird places like Benares, Perth, and Manila. It's like he's on a drug trip. I can't reason with him. Last month he cashed in thirty-two thousand dollars worth of securities, two weeks before they matured."

I looked up to see the man at the end of the bar standing, the girl at his side. He must have figured it out. He walked by and smiled, with his catch hanging onto his arm. Better hide your wallet, I thought.

"Dan, are you with me? I was telling you about Dr. West. The guy is totally irrational about his investments, and I have a tough time getting him to listen to my recommendations. Now that we've lost so much of his account, Jack's breathing down my neck. Just yesterday, he told me to do whatever it takes to get the doctor to stop withdrawing his cash."

Jack Walsh, president of AFR, usually gave his account managers a free hand, as long as he agreed with the decisions, but he was tough when he felt we weren't aggressive enough in maintaining our part of the business. I understood the pressure Ted was under.

"Now the doctor is back in town," he said. "But I think he's leaving at the end of the month. He wants someone to help him write a book about faith healing or something. When I met with him last Thursday, he tried to explain the reasons for his unusual behavior, but none of it makes any sense to me."

It should have been obvious I was irritated with Ted. I wasn't interested in his problems and didn't care if he had lost an account. I'd come to Boston to find work, expecting him to help. I wondered how I could make him understand without divulging too much information.

Ted ignored my frustration. "I don't know what the guy is thinking," he said. "It started with some medicine man performing miracle cures, and it's gone downhill for me ever since." He rolled his eyes. "Dr.

West even sold his practice to devote all his time to this project—whatever it is."

I leaped on an opportunity to explain what I wanted. "Maybe there's some way I could help you, do some consulting or something. I could work with other clients too. A little taste of the business might cure my boredom."

"No, it's my problem. I'll figure it out. I wasn't asking you to get involved. I appreciate the offer, but I just needed to vent. Besides, I've got a better idea. I can't believe you called when you did. I should have thought of you, but it has been four years. If Dr. West wants to write about his experiences, who could help him better than you?

"He'll spend whatever it takes to get his message out. He told me he wants to take a more professional approach and avoid being included with all the New Age nonsense that's out there, but he has no writing experience. He'll need a lot of help. I think he's already talked with a couple of writers, but as far as I know, he hasn't chosen anyone yet.

"Dan, you need to talk to him. I'll help if you're interested."

Ted caught me off guard, completely ignoring my original intent. I hadn't come to Boston looking for a writing assignment. That was the last thing I wanted.

"I'm sorry Ted, but I'm not interested. I'm no ghostwriter. In fact, I'm not much of a writer at all. I came here to—"

"Who are you kidding?" Ted paused and wrinkled his face. "I remember the proposals you used to write. You could sell oil in Kuwait. Remember the Union Retirement Fund and how we almost lost them? Their investment had declined by over a half-million dollars. I don't remember what you wrote them, but they kept their account with us and even invested more money. Don't give me that false modesty bit. I've seen your writing."

"Ted, you don't understand." And I wasn't ready to offer an explanation. My failures were too painful to discuss and had caused me to lose my desire to write. I was more trapped than I'd ever been in my old job, but I needed to return to that life, having failed to find success away from it.

"Maybe you don't need the money," he answered. His voice indicated more understanding than I found comfortable. "But it could be interesting work."

He looked at me for a moment as if he were unsure what to say next. His expression showed concern. He picked up his cocktail napkin, rolled it into a tight cylinder, and began tapping lightly on the bar—a nervous habit I remembered from years earlier.

"Dan," he said. "This could be the opportunity you need, the exposure you've been looking for. Don't say no without giving yourself a chance to see if you can really do it. You know you have the ability. Don't trip over your ego trying to hide your fear. You would be great."

My face grew hot and I slammed my glass to the bar. "Dammit!" I said. My voice was louder than intended. "You don't know what you're talking about."

Ted frowned. "Okay," he said. "I'm not trying to force you into something you're not interested in, but you're right for this job. Hell, you're perfect. You have the persistence, talent, and ability to hold a project together better than anyone I know. Maybe it's not what you're accustomed to or what you'd like, but it might be interesting work. But if you don't want it," Ted rolled another napkin and held it in front of him. His voice dropped to a whisper. "That's fine."

I faced the bar and emptied my glass. Neither of us spoke. After an uncomfortable silence, Ted looked at his watch.

"I have to go," he said. "Sorry if I offended you. It was good to see you again. Call me if you change your mind." He gave a half-smile, slipped off his stool, and was gone.

Hell no, I wasn't interested. I'd been looking for a strategy that would get me back into the business. I didn't need to waste more time writing, and I didn't want some mindless charity job. "Bartender, empty glass here."

A couple of refills later Ted's words were still rattling around in my head. Of course he'd been right, but that didn't make it easier to accept. What if my ego sometimes got in the way and I made decisions based upon appearance? I'd always been that way. Wasn't everyone?

I left Riordan's and walked across the street. When I reached Northern Avenue, I turned east and went down to the piers. For more than an hour I watched the planes across the harbor at Logan. The irony of Ted's proposal was incredible. I needed work. There were bills to pay. I should have listened to him.

It was too late to look for a room, and I needed to save the money anyway. I walked to the car and started for Wareham. My mind was numb. Was it the alcohol or Ted's probing? I didn't care.

The next morning a jackhammer worked inside my head while my mind replayed the words of the previous night. I knew Ted was trying to be helpful and I'd "tripped over my ego," as he described it. I thought about his proposal. Ghost writing, not the most glamorous or rewarding type of writing, but writers sometimes do it and are paid well. I was certain I could get the job if I wanted it.

I took a sip of coffee, swallowed my pride, and picked up the phone.

CHAPTER 3

THE ODYSSEY BEGINS

"Ted, this is Dan. Sorry about last night. I had a little too much to drink. I didn't mean to sound ungrateful. I'd like to meet your doctor friend if the offer still stands. The job sounds interesting."

"Great. It's strange you called. I just hung up with him. He's coming in tomorrow at three. Can you be here?"

"Yeah, I think so," I said. I tried not to sound too eager. "Three should be okay."

"Why don't you come about thirty minutes early so I can fill you in on what I know about Dr. West." Ted was being his usual, helpful self.

"Okay," I said. "Two-thirty it is. Thanks again, Ted. I appreciate your help."

"And by the way," he paused. "I've moved to the third floor now . . . uh . . . in your old office. See you tomorrow."

My old office, I thought. It appeared I'd trained him well. I was happy for him, but could feel the muscles tighten in my stomach.

I spent the afternoon wondering about the doctor and his mystery job. Though it could be the break I needed, the chance was probably slim. I wondered how much it would pay.

****

It was 2:05 when I arrived at Ted's office. I spent the extra time browsing at the corner newsstand. I didn't want to seem too enthusiastic and didn't want to sit in the outer office making small talk with Kay. Even if she had forgiven me for not calling, I didn't want to face the inevitable questions about the past four years.

As the clock approached 2:30, I walked to the entrance of AFR, pausing before the big brass door that had greeted me for fourteen years. I no longer felt welcome, a stranger in an alien environment. I pulled on the door and stepped inside.

As I turned the corner towards Ted's office, I saw Kay, sitting behind the familiar mahogany desk. She looked up and smiled as I approached. "May I help you?"

27

Her smile changed to bewilderment as I drew near. "Dan," she gasped. She sat expressionless for a moment, then regained her composure and smiled once more. "Dan, it's good to see you. How are you?"

"I'm fine. Good to see you too," I said. I fumbled with my watch. "I'm here to see Ted. I have a two-thirty appointment."

"He's in his office. Go on in."

I hurried towards Ted's open door. I don't think I've ever felt more uncomfortable.

Ted looked up from behind my old desk and stood to greet me, teeth gleaming in a broad smile. "Dan, I'm glad you could make it a little early. Let me tell you what I know about Dr. West and what he's up to."

He walked over and shook my hand. "Have a seat. I think you'll be glad you reconsidered. You'll enjoy meeting the doctor. He's a nice guy; at least he used to be. I called him after I spoke with you yesterday and told him you'd be here. I explained how you'd been the brains behind this outfit for almost fifteen years and how you gave it up to become a writer. He seemed interested when I said you might be able to offer some pointers to help him get started with his book. Of course, I think you should write the book, but I didn't say that. It would be better if he figured that out on his own."

I sat down in one of the big leather chairs across from Ted and leaned back. The leather felt softer, more comfortable than I remembered from when the chairs had been purchased about eight years before.

"Thanks, Ted. I'm sorry about what happened at Riordan's; hope I didn't offend you. There's been a lot of pressure lately. I do appreciate your help."

"I understand," he said. "but don't thank me yet. This may be too strange to work, but you won't know until you talk with him.

"By the way, I'd appreciate it if you'd put in a good word for me when you're talking with the doctor. I hope he'll get through this diversion with at least some of his funds intact. Maybe I can get him to rebuild his account with us. And if you help him generate book profits, he might need my advice on new investments too. So give him your best shot, okay?"

Ted reminded me of my old self, always looking for a sales opportunity.

During the next few minutes, Ted gave me what little information he had about the book Dr. West wanted to write. Unfortunately, it was little more than I already knew. Ted didn't understand alternative healing and was skeptical about the book. He was more interested in giving me the latest news from the world of investing and in quizzing me about the past four years.

"I heard about you and Susan," he said. "Sorry. You two always seemed to be great together. I guess I never saw the whole picture, huh?"

When it came to Susan, I'd never seen the whole picture either. We had met in high school and dated through college. She seemed perfect—beautiful, intelligent, and caring. In the beginning she'd been supportive, interested in everything I did. Why had she changed?

She said she wanted children, wanted a more normal life. I wanted a family too, but the time was never right. The long hours I worked weren't only for me. Surely she understood that. She spent the money easily enough.

I stared out the window and recalled a few lines from a poem:

> ". . . What happened
> to the one I loved?
> Where did she go?
> Gone away, perhaps
> to seek the one
> she loved."

I turned towards Ted. "Yeah," I said. "You never know. I suppose some of it was my fault. After I left the company, money became an issue. And I needed time to myself. I was busy with several writing projects and spent a lot of time alone at our place at Marblehead. When I was home, I was usually in my study."

"I read the *Financial News* article you did," Ted said. "I thought it was great. We passed it around the office and everyone talked about how we all knew you before you became famous."

"How's the little one?" I asked. I couldn't remember his child's name.

"He's fine. Brent's not so little though. He just turned five and recently announced he wants to become a plumber when he grows up. Yeah, a couple of months ago we added a bath in the basement, and Brent was fascinated with all the tools and stuff. And with what the guy charged me, I think I'll encourage him."

Kay's voice interrupted on the intercom. "Dr. West is here to see you."

"Send him in," Ted said. We stood to greet him.

The doctor was not at all as I'd envisioned. I'd imagined him to appear eccentric and unconventional, but the guy standing before us looked like a Marine, younger than I'd expected, clean-cut and conservative.

"Dr. West," Ted spoke. "I'd like you to meet Dan Murphy."

"Hello, Dr. West," I said.

The doctor gripped my hand. "Please call me Mike," he said. "You've got quite a reputation around here, Dan. The way Ted describes it, you're responsible for most of AFR's past success. Sorry I didn't have an opportunity to meet you before you left."

We made small talk for several minutes and I liked him almost immediately. He was more natural and unpretentious than I had envisioned, yet with an unusual confidence. I wondered if his experiences had changed him. I was comfortable talking with him and wondered what it would be like helping with his book.

"Ted tells me you're a writer," Dr. West spoke. "Quite a good one. I'd like to discuss some ideas I have for a book, but I'm sure Ted has better things to do than listen to me ramble on. Would it be possible for you to come up to my place at Devereaux Beach tomorrow? I know it's short notice, but I'll be leaving town in a few days and would appreciate any help you can give me. I'm having a difficult time getting started. Everything I write seems so dry and boring. I don't think anyone would want to read it."

"Yes," I said, "I suppose I can, but I'm not sure I can be of much assistance."

"Any help would be appreciated. You'll come then?"

We agreed to meet the next day at 10:00 A.M. After he gave me directions, I excused myself and left them to conduct their business.

On the way out I paused at Kay's desk. "Sorry I never called. I didn't know what to say. The past few years have been pretty strange."

"I know," she said. Her eyes told me she understood. "It was good to see you again."

"Maybe we can have dinner sometime and talk about the good old days," I said. Inside, I felt there was little chance of that happening.

"I'd really like that." She smiled and nodded her head.

We were interrupted by Ted's voice on the intercom. "Kay, would you bring me Dr. West's current file?"

"I'll let you get to work," I said. "Can't keep the boss waiting. It was good to see you." I turned to go down the hall.

31

"See you later," she called.

As I waited for the elevator I thought about Kay, wishing we could have talked longer. During the past few years I'd blocked her out of my thoughts. At that moment, however, I realized I cared for her more than I'd been willing to admit, and I hurried to get out of the building.

The wind caught me by surprise as I stepped onto the sidewalk. It seemed colder and reminded me of mornings at Marblehead. God, I loved that place. The decision to sell it had been difficult. It wasn't that I'd had a choice; it was either sell or starve.

My mind painted a picture of Kay sitting with me on the porch, listening to the water crash against the rocks, and watching the sun disappear behind the trees. I wished she could have seen it before it was gone. But the prospect of meaningful work captured my attention, and I spent the afternoon thinking about how I was going to convince the doctor to let me help him.

****

The next morning, I drove up to Dr. West's, still thinking about Kay. I wanted to call her, but doubts filled my mind. What if she wasn't interested in renewing our friendship? Maybe she was just being nice. When I reached the house, I was still undecided about making the call.

As I turned onto the drive, maneuvering between two large stone columns, someone stumbled directly into my path. I spun the wheel and slammed on the brakes. At first, I thought it was a child, but as my car skidded to a halt in the flowerbed, I saw it was a young woman, probably in her late twenties and dressed in a white robe.

I leaped from the car. "Are you okay?" I asked.

"Sorry," she said, "I've been doing my morning meditation in the garden. It always makes me a little lightheaded. You must be Mr. Murphy. I'm Paula West."

I shook her outstretched hand. "Yes, I'm Dan Murphy. Sorry about the pansies. Glad you weren't hurt."

"No problem. I'm protected," she said and smiled. "I think my husband is in his study. I'll show you in."

Mike West was seated at a large roll-top desk as we entered the room. "Mr. Murphy is here," his wife announced. "He thinks he almost ran over me in the driveway." She laughed. "I told him I'm protected."

The study was perfect. The walls were golden oak paneling, rich and impressive. One wall, probably sixteen feet long, was filled with books. Across the room, the opposite wall was entirely of glass and looked out upon a meadow and the forest beyond. The view was spectacular.

"Good morning, Dan. Would you like some tea?"

"No thanks. I stopped at Walden's for one of their special breakfasts. I used to be a regular there. I had a place in Marblehead."

Paula excused herself and skipped out of the room. She seemed a little flaky. What did she mean, "protected?"

"You have to get used to Paula's enthusiasm," her husband said. "She has a view of life that few can understand. Three years ago, she was pronounced clinically dead."

"What?" I asked.

"I'll tell you about that later, but first you have to hear my story." The doctor pulled up a chair facing his and leaned forward. "Have a seat," he said.

"Do you know anything about healing, non-medical healing?" he asked. "Some refer to it as spiritual or psychic healing."

"Yes," I answered. "I'm familiar with spiritual healing. A few years ago I was interested in the various forms of psychic phenomena, including healing. I read some of the so-called cures. I was looking for some mystical clue to explain my life and explored a number of metaphysical disciplines over a period of several years. My interest waned when it became clear that none of the teachings held the answers I was seeking."

"The things I've seen might change your mind," he said. "During the past three years, I've learned some healing techniques, non-medical and very unconventional, that the average person would regard as miraculous. I want to make those techniques available to the general public. My goal is to accomplish this in a two-stage approach."

"Miracles? What do you mean?"

"Yeah, some call them miracles, but I believe there's a scientific basis for the cures. I'm working to incorporate some unusual healing techniques into traditional medicine. There have been many cases where conventional medicine has given up, but where cures were later affected without any involvement from the medical community. Such cases form the basis of my research.

"My plan is to increase awareness of these remarkable healing methods by writing and promoting a book that will outline a new approach to healing. I want to describe what I've observed in a way that is believable so that my claims won't be dismissed as false or fanatical."

"That may be more difficult than you imagine," I said. "Won't you have to present your findings to the medical community prior to any exposure to the general public? You'll need the AMA's stamp of approval, won't you?"

"Yes, to a certain extent, but I'm not willing to wait for acceptance from the AMA. It would take years to do the kind of study necessary for their approval, and there are many who wouldn't accept the findings even when they were proven beyond a doubt. I don't plan to waste my efforts trying to convince a bunch of skeptics. I already have some support. Others will join me when they see the interest we'll generate. That interest will be created by the book and through a series of healing centers I plan to develop that will make non-traditional healing available to anyone needing and desiring treatment, regardless of their financial means. The centers will be staffed by medical professionals who have been trained in both traditional and alternative medicine.

"Time is critical to the success of my efforts and the information must be disseminated quickly. Lives are at stake."

I turned and looked out the window. Paula was walking across the meadow. She seemed to float along the path.

"What information?" I asked. The skepticism in my voice was obvious. "And why is it so critical?"

"Let me tell you a story," he began. "A story I couldn't believe the first time I heard it.

"Several years ago, a young girl was hospitalized in the final stages of cancer of the liver. Her disease had metastasized into other organs and she'd become comatose. Knowing that death was near, the doctors called in the girl's family and told them she wouldn't survive more than a few days."

Dr. West shifted in his chair and pulled at his lip. I felt he was searching for a way to help me understand and believe.

35

"As often happens," he said, "one of the nurses assigned to the girl had become emotionally attached. When she realized the doctors had given up, the nurse decided to try a rather unorthodox treatment. She had a friend who also practiced medicine, but not the kind we normally accept. Some would call this person a shaman or medicine man. Anyway, at the nurse's request, and with the permission of the girl's family, the healer came to the hospital and performed a healing ritual on her."

I looked out the window again. Paula was standing at a large flowering bush near the edge of their garden. Butterflies were flying around her. I watched as she raised her arms, palms upward, allowing several of the colorful creatures to alight in her hands.

Mike West paused and looked at his wife. "She talks to them," he said. "She has much more wisdom than I do, but I'm learning."

He continued his story as if there was nothing unusual about the scene we were watching. "The next morning, the girl sat up in bed for the first time in weeks. Her doctors, of course, assumed some type of temporary remission, and for a day or so, didn't bother trying to determine if her actual condition had changed. However, after several days of the girl's continued improvement, new tests were ordered." He paused again.

I was still looking at Paula. She seemed to have stirred a memory I couldn't identify. For a moment the area around her seemed to grow brighter, and as I stared, my vision blurred. I shook my head and blinked several times. I wondered what she knew, wondered if she had reached the state of awareness I'd once sought.

"You may have already guessed the results." Mike's voice startled me and I looked towards him, unable to bring my eyes into focus. He ignored my obvious discomfort and continued. "All signs of the previous cancer were gone and, although weak, the girl appeared to be in almost perfect health."

I tried to concentrate on what he was saying.

"Believe it or not," he said. "That's exactly what happened."

"Uh . . . I believe you," I said. "It's just that". . . I paused, unable to describe what I'd been feeling and it had nothing to do with his story. "Please continue."

"I'm familiar with this case," he said. "Because the doctor who made the original diagnosis is my brother. He called me, not only because he knew I would have a professional interest, but also because my previous wife died from the same type of cancer."

"Aren't there many such cases of spontaneous remission?" I asked.

"Yes, that's what makes it so interesting and important. The medical community has always dismissed such cases as inexplicable anomalies, and that's true. Traditional medicine can't explain them, but that doesn't mean there isn't an explanation, just not one we understand.

"Now, after a couple of years of research, studying hundreds of different cases, I think I have sufficient information to go public. I don't have all the answers, but I know it's possible to replicate a lot more of the cures than we're currently doing. I've met some gifted and unusual people and have seen dozens of cases, probably more than anyone, of instantaneous cures of many so-called incurable diseases."

Mike stood and walked over to his bookshelves, pointing to several rows of books. "There are more cases here like the one I just described. The difference is that most of these were written by lay people, loosely associated with medicine. That's why they have had such a difficult time being widely accepted. I plan a different approach. My credentials and the support of others within the medical community will, I hope, add a new dimension to the literature on alternative healing.

"In the girl's case I actually met the shaman who treated the her. It turned out he had a regular practice—if you can call it that—and he continues to treat and cure many illnesses where conventional practitioners have given up.

"One of the problems I face is that traditional medicine is no different from other disciplines and, I'm afraid, will fight vigorously to protect its interests. Several in the alternative medicine community have already been prosecuted for the illegal practice of medicine. I'm sure we'll have opposition from the AMA."

"Can't you avoid that by simply getting the information to licensed physicians?" I asked.

"Unfortunately, that's the Gordian knot of this situation. Many practicing physicians will find this information too incredible to investigate. You must remember that it goes against everything we've been taught. And those who may be interested will fear reprisals from the AMA.

"Somehow we—and I hope you want to help with this—we'll have to present the information in a way that causes the public to pressure the medical establishment to both investigate and embrace as a part of their regimen."

I glanced out the window. Paula had disappeared. I could see how Mike West could be attracted to her. She seemed to embody the essence of what he was attempting to pull together, in touch with a reality far removed from the temporal. But her story and others like it, however remarkable they might be, would never be enough to overcome the skeptics. He would have to do much more than present interesting stories. I wondered how many of his cures could be verified scientifically. The task would be a challenge.

"How do you plan to present your case?" I asked. "Keeping it separated from the vacuous nonsense that's out there won't be easy. The public is generally suspicious of claims such as yours, although I think they would like to believe in them. I'm sure the medical establishment will be far more skeptical."

"To begin with," Mike said. "I'll cite cases where scientific and medical verification has already been established. Many doctors participate in such cases each year, observing miraculous and inexplicable cures, yet they never try to understand the basis for recovery. Their training has been deficient in offering an explanation or even discussing such phenomena. They categorize them as spontaneous remission, making no effort to discover the root cause.

"However, a growing number of physicians," he continued, "have begun to question the unwillingness of medical schools to provide an explanation. I hope my work will force the medical establishment to re-evaluate its limited position. My long-term wish would be a movement toward an era of open-mindedness and inquiry."

I thought about my potential reputation as a writer. "What if the book proves nothing?" I asked. "What if you're merely labeled as another zealot who's been duped by the lunatic fringe?"

"I'm willing to take that risk, but I don't think we can seriously discuss the possibilities until you can see firsthand what I'm describing. That's why I'd like for you to go to Arizona with me and see a healing center that's already in operation. Then, perhaps we can develop our approach. I'm leaving for Phoenix the first of June. Could you join me for a few days? I'll pay your expenses, of course."

"I'm between projects right now," I said. "Maybe I could come for a day or two, but I can't guarantee I'll be able to help."

"I'm not asking for a guarantee. I'd just like you to experience some of the things I've seen. Perhaps you can show me how to describe the experiences on paper. I assure you it won't be a waste of your time."

"Give me a few days," he said. "You'll see. If what I've told you is true and what you see is real, the experience could be life changing. On the other hand, if I'm just a crackpot doctor, gone off the deep end, then the worst that can happen is you get a few days in a beautiful setting at my expense. What do you say?"

"Let me think about it. I'll have to admit, you've aroused my curiosity."

"Good. I don't want to sound presumptuous, but I believe you'll accept."

He stood and clasped his hands around mine. "Think about it and give me a call. But I'll need your answer by Friday."

He continued to grasp my hand and looked into my eyes. I felt he was looking for something more than confirmation. And though I should have been ecstatic about the possibility of a job, I was apprehensive, confused by the strange turn of events.

"I'll call you," I said. I pulled away and went out the door.

CHAPTER 4

DISTORTED REALITY

I spent the following week at the library, going through everything they had on alternative healing. I also browsed through a couple of metaphysical bookstores. I'd decided on the drive home from the West's that I would, as Mike had predicted, accept the offer to accompany him to Phoenix. Ted was right. It might pay the bills—at least some of them. Why should I care if the concept was screwy?

It was astonishing to discover the number of books written about non-medical healing. People seemed hungry for information that wasn't being provided by traditional medicine.

There were books about Native American healing rituals, the healing power of prayer, touch therapy, obscure methods such as pranic healing, and numerous related topics. I was amazed, but skeptical.

It wasn't surprising to discover that the information available was inconclusive, failing to provide concrete measures by which such cures could be repeated. And many of the books were too esoteric to be understood by the general public. However, I was impressed by the sheer volume of the work and felt that more study was probably warranted.

I wondered how so much could be written about a subject with universal interest, and yet be accepted by only a relative few. I was sure Dr. West had a more difficult task than he imagined.

When I phoned to accept his offer, Paula answered. "Dan, it's good to hear from you. I suppose you called to tell Mike that you'll accompany us to Phoenix, right?"

"Well, uh . . . yes I did. Do you read minds too?"

"Oh, it's just a little technique we learned in the Philippines. It's really not that unusual. We listen with our hearts instead of our ears," she said.

"Okay, if you say so. Is your husband in?"

"No, he's at a conference in New York. He'll be home tomorrow."

"Please ask him to call me when he returns."

"Of course," she said. "I look forward to seeing you again. Maybe you'll want to learn to listen with your heart too."

"For now," I responded. "I'll be content if it just keeps beating. So, you're going to Phoenix?"

"Yes, I accompany Mike on most of his trips. He says it helps him remain open to new ideas and gives him a different perspective."

Yes, I thought, I'll bet it does give him a different perspective—a very different perspective.

"Well, I guess I'll see you in two weeks," I said. "Please ask Mike to call me."

I hung up remembering Dr. West had failed to tell me the story about Paula being declared clinically dead, and I'd forgotten to ask what she meant by "protected." It didn't matter; I'd have plenty of time to find out later.

****

As I searched for information on alternative healing, I tried to find as many books as possible similar to the concept Dr. West was proposing. I wondered how much competition we would have and hoped to improve both my understanding and vocabulary of metaphysical terminology.

My search led me to rediscover metaphysical works I'd read years before, re-igniting my questions regarding man's relationship to a higher power. Though I tried to ignore everything that seemed unrelated to my task, it was difficult to overlook the vast amount of new material with which I was totally unfamiliar. I wondered if there was some underlying purpose and questioned the unusual series of coincidences that had guided me to the doctor and his proposed book.

One day before our departure, I was browsing through a small bookstore, looking for reading material to take on the trip, when I picked up a magazine on alternative healing. I recalled the pages I'd found on my boat, a story about healing. I tried to remember what I'd done with them.

I purchased a couple of paperbacks and hurried back to the boat to locate the article. As I drove, I became obsessed with finding it. The more I thought how silly my actions were, the more determined I became. However, I had no idea what I'd done with the article, didn't remember seeing it after returning from my trip, and feared I might have tossed it out.

My search lasted more than an hour, and I was ready to give up when I found the pages tucked inside my chart folder. I walked over to the dinette and sat down. The story was a group of anecdotes about people who had survived serious illness and who attributed their recoveries to non-medical healing. A quick glance told me that it was more of the stuff I'd been reading for the past couple of weeks. I was disappointed and wondered why I'd been so preoccupied with finding it. I folded the pages and began to pack my bag. I could read on the flight.

****

Traffic to Logan airport was terrible, as usual. As I rode the tram to the terminal, I wondered if this project was the opportunity I'd been seeking. Perhaps I was wasting my time with this eccentric doctor. Was I realistic in thinking I could write something about healing that would be dramatically different from all other writings to date? I didn't think so.

As I approached the departure gate, I glanced at my watch. It was 2:30. Forty-five minutes until our flight. I paced back and forth across the concourse, developing serious doubts about the trip.

By the time Mike and Paula arrived, I'd convinced myself I'd made a mistake, that I should never have agreed to join them. However, my questioning was quickly forced to a halt as they approached. "Good afternoon, Dan," they spoke in unison.

The couple had the naively innocent look of newlyweds. Though they were young, their eyes conveyed the wisdom and tranquility that seems to come with age. Something about them caused my doubts to fade, and my focus returned to my new adventure.

We boarded the plane and shuffled down the aisle. Mike turned to me and grinned. "Remember I promised to tell you about Paula's experience? Since she's here, she can tell you."

Paula was like a little child, eager to divulge a secret. As soon as we'd taken our seats, she began.

"Dan, I understand you're interested in my story," she said. "It started when I was a child. My mother had been killed in an automobile accident when I was four, and I was sent to live with my father's sister, Polly. Although my aunt was kind and loving, she was much older than my mother and, I think, somewhat uncomfortable meeting the needs of a four-year-old. I spent a lot of time alone. But I wasn't unhappy. I always felt I was special, different from the other kids, but in a good way, and I had a secret friend named Anna.

"Shortly after mother died, Anna appeared to me. She came one night when I was sleeping, woke me, and held me in her arms. I don't know why, but I wasn't afraid. I welcomed her, sensing the same loving presence I'd felt from my mom. Anna helped me cope with the trauma of mother's death. Although she was much older than I was, we were like best friends, laughing and playing together.

"Sometimes she'd be serious and talk about God and things I barely understood. She corrected me when I was rude or impolite, but never scolded. She taught me to consider how I might feel if someone did the same thing to me."

"You saw her," I interrupted, "just as you see me now?"

"Yes, as clearly as I see you and Mike. For a long time I didn't realize I was the only one who could see and hear Anna, and when I became aware of the uniqueness of my vision, I knew not to share it with anyone."

"But most children have imaginary playmates," I said. "Why do you think your vision was different?"

"Anna wasn't a figment of my imagination. She regularly told me things I would have no other way of knowing, once warning me that my aunt would become ill and have to be hospitalized. She said I would have to stay with my grandparents who lived in another city. But Anna told me not to be concerned, that my aunt would soon recover and I would return home. Within a week, it all happened as Anna had predicted, and because she had prepared me, I wasn't frightened when my grandfather came to pick me up.

"Sometimes, when I was around others, Anna stood aside and observed, later commenting on my actions and explaining the actions of those I'd been with. It seemed normal to me. I really didn't think much about how she fit into my life. She was just there."

Paula's story was intriguing, but sounded like dozens of others that have formed the plots for interesting magazine articles and television shows. However, her story was taking me to the limits of my beliefs, and I was having difficulty accepting everything she said.

My face must have betrayed my doubts, because Paula gripped my arm and said, "Wait, it gets better.

"Anna spent several years with me, explaining how God was not an old man on a throne, meting out rewards and punishment, but is a loving presence I could have with me always. Anna said I was a part of God, that if I would sit quietly and think about Him, I could feel God inside me."

As we sped down the runway, I silently regretted we'd been able to get adjoining seats.

"Excuse me," Paula said. She turned to Mike and leaned her head on his shoulder.

For a couple of minutes I thought I'd had a reprieve, but when we had gained altitude, she turned back to me. "Sorry," she said. "I love flying, but takeoff always makes me a little uneasy. Now, where was I?

"Oh, I remember. As I grew older, Anna began to prepare me for life as an adult, sometimes leaving me for days or even weeks. Each time she returned she asked if I'd been feeling God inside me. Sometimes I'd have to admit I'd forgotten, but I recall her response as clearly as if she were still here. I can only be with you for a short time, she'd remind me, but the God within would be with me always."

Paula was interrupted by the pilot's announcement giving our altitude and expected arrival time. The flight should be smooth, he said, and weather conditions in Arizona sounded like a nice change from the wind and rain Boston had recently experienced. I was eager to get to Phoenix to see what Mike's healing center had to offer and ready for Paula's story to end.

The pilot had hardly finished, however, when Paula continued. "When I was twelve, Anna said she would be leaving, that I no longer needed her. I was sad and cried for a few minutes, but somehow I knew she was right. It was time for her to go. When she left, nothing special happened; she told me she loved me, reminded me to love myself and others, then turned and walked away."

"Was that the end of it?" I asked.

"No, not at all. It's only the beginning of the exciting part, but some other things happened first.

"As time passed, I thought less and less about Anna, placing her with my other childhood memories." Paula twisted in her seat to face me.

"So, you ask. What does this have to do with being saved from death?"

No, that wasn't what I would have asked. I wanted to be convinced, to understand what made Paula's story different. I looked toward Mike. He was reading a magazine and seemed oblivious to our conversation.

I turned back to Paula. I wondered if she really believed her story. She seemed unaware of my doubts.

"This is where it gets good," she said. "A little more than three years ago, I was diagnosed with a rare form of leukemia, and the doctors gave me only a few months to live. I was devastated. I cried, prayed, and cursed my fate. In less than a month I began to lose my strength, and by the end of the forth month, I had to be hospitalized. I was, as they say, a 'goner.'

"After a couple of weeks in the hospital, I was in so much pain I was receiving massive doses of painkiller. I was barely conscious and wanted to die. The night I died, I'd asked God to take me. I couldn't endure the suffering. At some point the pain stopped, and I remember a nurse coming into my room, checking my pulse, and running out. Later, I was told the doctors had pronounced me dead."

I glanced out the window. Through breaks in the clouds I could see the mountains below coming alive with the brilliant green of spring. I wished I was off the plane. Paula made me uncomfortable. Though I wanted her to stop, I was captivated, drawn to her story like an animal to a trap.

"As you can see," she continued, "the doctors were wrong. I remember seeing a bright light and felt I was moving through a long, narrow tunnel. As I neared the end of the tunnel, the light was so bright I couldn't look at it. I thought I was seeing God. I didn't think about being dead; I didn't feel dead. I was seeing, experiencing things that were incredible. After I'd been there for a time—I have no idea how long—I saw people. Some of them talked to me, but not in words. They communicated through their thoughts.

"I was shown events from my life, times when I didn't respond with the highest good of the situation in mind, but I didn't see with my eyes. The things I saw weren't visible in a physical sense, but everything was incredibly clear. Everything had purpose. My experience caused me to feel a great sadness, and I felt guilty for the things I'd done. However, I wasn't being judged. I experienced how my actions had caused pain and suffering and I judged myself."

"Sounds like a classic near-death experience," I said. "I've read about them. Many researchers believe the lights you see are only the random firings of a brain starved for oxygen."

"It was real for me. I'm not interested in what the skeptics say. I don't think the cause makes a difference. The scientists didn't have my experience. What I felt, what I know, was wonderful. I saw Anna. She came to me and told me I couldn't stay there, that it wasn't yet my time.

"Anna said I would return to help with the healing of the world, that she would come with me and help me. I didn't want to leave and begged her to let me stay. In that place I felt incredible peace and love, but as I describe the feeling, I know it sounds trite.

Anyway, Anna said I must return, and in a short time, I felt myself being pushed back into the tunnel. I seemed to be flying through space and soon found myself back in my hospital room. I could see my body lying on the bed and my father beside me, holding my hand and crying. I felt great compassion for him and understood the love and the loss he was experiencing.

"My vision faded and I felt a jolt as I returned to my body. My father later told me I raised up and cried out for Anna."

Paula looked at me and frowned. "You don't believe me, do you?"

My face flushed. "Well, yes. I believe you're being honest, that is, I believe you think you experienced those things."

"The doctors sure thought it was real," she said. "Within a week, they couldn't find a trace of disease in my body and I began to regain my strength. I left the hospital a week later."

"That's amazing." I feigned more interest than I felt. "I've heard about such cases, but you're the first dead person I've met."

I stood. "If you'll excuse me, I better make a break for it before they block the aisle with the refreshment cart."

Mike seemed engrossed in his magazine and ignored me as I stepped into the aisle. I wanted to get away from Paula. Her story was interesting, but what did it prove? Could it possibly benefit anyone else?

Once in the restroom I closed the door and began to remove my jacket when something fell to the floor. It was the article I'd brought, the one I'd found on my boat. I gathered up the pages, putting them in order. *Psychic Healing—Myth or Miracle*, the title read. My eyes were drawn to a small picture at the bottom of page three. As I focused on the picture, I gasped. It was Paula West! The caption read: "Guardian angel brings girl back from the dead." I could hardly hold the article as I read on.

The article recounted how the doctors were so puzzled by Paula's miraculous recovery that she was tested at the prestigious Massachusetts Institute for Advance Medicine. She'd even been featured on the local news. It seemed that part of her story was true. Even the doctors were impressed.

Much more than her strange recovery, though, I was completely bewildered by the bizarre events that had given me Paula's story, long before I had met her. What was happening to me, and why? My mind returned to my ordeal at sea—I still wasn't sure what had happened out there. Had the stranger been real? How could he have known, seen something in my future that hadn't even begun to unfold?

A chill ran through my body as I pondered the questions and the implications. I leaned on the sink and splashed cold water on my face. Several minutes passed before I stuffed the article back into my pocket and returned to my seat. I didn't mention what had happened.

"You okay?" Mike asked. "You look a little green."

"Flying," I said. "Sometimes doesn't agree with me."

"Want to know what happened to Anna?" Paula asked. She didn't wait for an answer.

"Anna really did come back with me," she said. "I talk with her sometimes, although I don't see her as I did when I was a child. She's helped Mike and me learn about some wonderful healers."

"That's . . . uh . . . that's nice," I said.

Mike stuffed his magazine into the seat pocket. "I know what Paula told you seems unbelievable," he said. "But don't make a quick judgment. You'll hear some amazing stories during the next few days."

CHAPTER 5

JOURNEY
THROUGH HEALING

I had no idea how prophetic Mike's words were until I'd been in Phoenix for a couple of days. As we drove from the airport, Mike told me about the Center and how he had discovered it a couple of years before. The facility was located about twenty miles from the city near the Sierra Estrella Mountains, an area of spectacular views and vegetation unexpected in such a harsh environment. The grounds were beautifully manicured, providing a tranquil setting for reflection and healing. I was impressed with the way the staff seemed to connect with the patients or, "guests" as they called them.

"I'll show you to your room," Mike said, as he directed me down the hall. "We're staying in the regular guest rooms. The visitor quarters are full, and anyway, I thought it would be good if you could experience the same environment as the guests. I want to let Dr. Won know we're here; I'll be back in a few minutes."

My room was small, but bright and cheerful. One wall opened onto a courtyard with a pond and fountain in the center. Looking at the pond, I reflected upon the circumstances that had brought me to Phoenix. It seemed strange I'd called Ted when I had. I wondered if the bizarre events of the recent past were related. Paula's story, my writing, the stranger—could it all be coincidence?

I lay on the bed staring at the ceiling. Whatever the cause, I wasn't going to argue with fate. The opportunity might bring me some recognition and some money.

Mike's knock on the door startled me. I'd been lost in thought. "I want to take you to meet the man who developed the Center, Dr. Hyo Won," he said.

As we walked down the hall, Mike explained that Dr. Won had studied Oriental Medicine in Beijing and later attended Harvard, where he specialized in epidemiology and cancer. We turned a corner and Mike spoke, "There he is. The gentleman in the smock." Mike gestured toward a dark-haired, distinguished looking man, speaking with a group of "guests."

Dr. Won looked up and smiled as we approached. He greeted Mike. "Welcome, Dr. West. Is this the man who is to make us famous?"

"Well, not exactly." Mike said. "But I hope he can help legitimize our efforts. Dr. Won, I'd like to introduce Dan Murphy. I've been telling him about the Center."

Dr. Won shook my hand vigorously. "Very good to meet you, Dan. I am happy for you to visit our humble retreat "

I chuckled at Dr. Won's enthusiasm. "Thank you for allowing me to come here. Dr. West tells me you perform some unusual cures," I said. "I'm looking forward to seeing exactly what you do."

Dr. Won introduced me to each member of the group and, after asking permission from his guests, gave a brief description of their condition. After a few moments of discussion, Dr. Won excused himself from the others and joined us as we continued our tour. He seemed to be aware of everything going on at the Center. Although they currently had more than seventy-five patients, Dr. Won recognized each one and was familiar with the most intimate details of their condition.

As we toured the grounds, I was fascinated with the varied way he would react to each person we encountered. One might receive a touch on the shoulder and a word or two whispered in their ear, while another would be warmly embraced, introduced to us and briefly included in our conversation. Many of the patients, or guests, appeared to be in above average physical condition, although all were described as having been diagnosed with serious or even fatal illnesses. When I asked Dr. Won how such severely ill people were able to function in such a positive fashion, he responded with a couple of questions.

"How," he asked, "do you account for the ability of someone under the influence of a hypnotist to recall facts or information that would be impossible for them to do in a normal, waking state? Or, what can give a one-hundred pound woman the strength to lift an automobile off the injured body of her child?

"The answer, we believe, is that the body and the mind are connected in ways that we are only beginning to understand. The mind is—or can be—in touch with a power for healing and energy that is far beyond our ability to comprehend. We believe there is no condition or disease that cannot be overcome through the proper use of this power."

"Surely you're not successful in all cases, are you?" I asked.

"No, not by the outside world's interpretation of success. In some cases, guests may succumb to their disease. Certain individuals do not seem to be appropriate for our methods of treatment, but we do not see these as failures of our method, merely a lack of understanding on our part to properly interpret the messages from the body.

"Many times," he said. "We find that an individual may need to express an illness physically, in order to accomplish some higher purpose, a purpose in which we may not be able to participate. In those cases, we try to understand as much as possible in order to help the person gain insight into their condition and the underlying cause. Our task is to make the patient as comfortable as possible so that their attention may be focused upon reaching a state of enlightenment."

We entered the main building and walked down a long corridor. Dr. Won pointed out the dining area where, he told us, only natural, organic foods were served.

"Do you ever prescribe drugs or surgery as methods of cure?" I asked.

"No, we do not. We use foods, herbs, massage, acupuncture, and meditation to supplement the body's natural healing powers, and avoid those methods we consider unnatural.

"The goal of the Center is quite simple. We believe that our purpose is to assist those who come to us seeking help. However, it is not for us to decide the form such assistance may take. We work to bring our guests into a condition of understanding of the relationship between their body and mind and the greater mind, which is the universe. Many times that understanding is all that is necessary for them to achieve perfect health."

I was confused. "What is the importance of all the diet, exercise and meditation therapy?" I asked. "Why do you have to set a regimen of such therapy for each patient?"

"Ah, that is medicine for the mind. We do not say to our guests, 'look to your self for the answer to your illness,' but try to assist them in making a connection with their body. At the Center we utilize the methods with which we are familiar. We apply those treatments that are most appropriate for the conditions we observe. On occasion, the body may seek a physical expression of its inner turmoil. A meditation process helps our guests reach that portion of the mind that caused their body to seek disease as a method for expression."

"Are you saying that there is no value to surgery or drugs?" I asked.

"Oh no, of course not. Man has made discoveries in medicine that can be most beneficial. There are times when traditional medicine may be the appropriate choice, but we do not practice traditional medicine here. Many times, however, we are able to assist in calling forth the body's healing abilities to supplement other, more traditional treatments.

"If one experiences infection, synthetic drugs may kill the organism causing the problem, but I always encourage my guests to discover the internal cause that allowed the organism to manifest itself as disease. There is still much for us to learn. We ask our guests and our practitioners to maintain an open mind to all possibilities."

"How do you know what course to follow with each individual? We're all so different in our problems and our needs."

"Dr. Won wrinkled his brow. "We do not claim to have all the answers. There is much we do not understand. Our work is in its infancy, and we are only beginning to understand the questions we must ask."

Dr. Won glanced at his watch. "Please excuse me," he said. "I must attend to my guests. Dr. West tells me you will help with his book. Such a book coming from a respected physician as he, can do much to make people aware of our work here. Tomorrow, we can continue our discussion, and I will introduce you to more of our guests who can share their experiences with you."

He excused himself and scurried back to his work. As he left, I felt he'd attempted to make his explanation a little too simple. There were far too many unanswered questions. I was sure there was a scientific basis for their successes and their failures. However, it seemed I would have to wait to discover the answers to my questions.

The following morning I awoke with a blinding headache. I'd experienced similar headaches in the past, and when one occurred, it was overwhelming. I could hardly function. I climbed out of bed and fumbled through my suitcase for some painkiller, having learned years before to always have some available. I found the pills my doctor had prescribed during my last attack and tugged on the cap. The label indicated a dosage of two, so I poured out three and reached for some water. I stumbled back to bed and glanced at the clock: 6:15 A.M.

Mike had asked me to meet him in the dining hall at 7:30. I doubted I could make it. I waited to see if I might get some relief, but by

7:00, the pain had worsened, pulsating in my head and radiating down the back of my neck. I picked up the phone and dialed Mike's room.

"Sorry, but I don't think I can join you for breakfast," I said. "Migraine. I'll probably be out of commission all day. I usually have to sleep these things off."

"I'll come down and see if I can do something," he said.

"Don't bother, I've already taken three Migrex. I won't get any relief for several hours."

"I'll be there in a few minutes." He hung up the phone without saying anything else.

About fifteen minutes had passed when I heard a knock on the door. "Come in Mike," I called. "It's open."

"Good morning, Mr. Murphy." The voice was not Mike's. "Dr. West said you are feeling ill."

I turned to see Dr. Won entering the room. "It's nothing," I said. I felt a bit self-conscious. "Just a headache. I think I need a little rest."

"Perhaps I can help." He walked over and placed his left hand on my forehead. He slipped his right hand onto the back of my neck and closed his eyes.

I would have welcomed any help, but the doctor's actions seemed a little melodramatic. After all, what I had was a migraine, not exactly a life-threatening illness.

He maintained his position without speaking, occasionally altering the position of his hands and pressing lightly with the tips of his fingers. His hands, especially the one on my forehead, felt unusually warm.

After a few minutes, he spoke. "Your body is expressing much stress. Headache is a symptom of the inner turmoil you are experiencing, a signal. Now, that it has your attention, you must listen to what it is saying.

58

"If you listen, there will be no need for headache. However, in order to get the message, you must focus upon your body. Lay here quietly for thirty minutes, but do not sleep. Ask your body to tell you what you must do to relieve the turmoil. If you will listen, you will receive an answer and then headache will have served its purpose. I will return later."

As he was leaving he turned and said, "Remember to ask the question. If your mind wanders, okay. Observe thoughts, let them pass, and return to the question." He closed the door and I could hear him in conversation outside my room. Maybe he and Mike were talking about me. I didn't care.

I rolled over and closed my eyes, feeling strange, not so much from the headache, but from what had occurred. The pain was still there, but not as severe as it had been earlier.

Dr. Won had said to ask the question. Okay, I thought, show me that there is something to this. I was willing to try anything to be rid of the pain.

What was my body trying to tell me? If it was to get rid of the turmoil, I could accept that. I had more than enough for one person, but I couldn't turn it off. It wasn't something I could control.

What was the message? How could I control my thoughts? Control. That was a word I understood. I'd always tried to control everything in my life, and, for years, had done an admirable job. Some had referred to me as a control freak, but I didn't see that as negative. I needed to be in control, though I'd had little success during the past few years.

"Let go." The words appeared on a screen in my mind. Big, bold letters—LET GO—the phrase of the nineties. The words were not just in my mind, but permeated my entire body. LET GO resounded through my being. I studied each letter. L-E-T G-O. The simplicity was astounding.

Although I could see the truth of letting go—releasing my stress, anxieties, my need to be in control—I wasn't at all sure how to accomplish such a task. Intellectualizing and actualizing are far apart and a vast chasm must be crossed in order to merge one with the other.

A soft knock on my door brought my attention to the present. Dr. Won pushed the door open. "How is your headache? You are feeling better, yes?" He walked over to the bed and placed his hands on my head and neck.

"Ah, you ARE feeling better. You are learning to listen to your body. You are learning to LET GO of your fascination with things which have no importance."

"Yes, I feel better," I said. At that moment I became aware that my headache had almost gone. "Thank you. I don't know what you did, but I feel much better."

"I did nothing. You did everything. I only gave the suggestion you needed."

"Well, whatever you did worked. Thanks again."

"You will join us for breakfast?" he asked.

"Yes," I said. "I'll be there as soon as I get dressed."

As Dr. Won started out of the room, he stopped and pulled open the curtains. "It is a beautiful day," he said. "Today you shall see much beauty."

My mind reeled as he stepped into the hall, closing the door behind him. I thought about the events of the past hour. My headache was gone. I wondered if Dr. Won was responsible or if I'd somehow cured myself? Perhaps the answer didn't matter, but I was fascinated by the process.

I took a quick shower, dressed, and hurried down to the dining hall. The air was filled with the aroma of freshly baked bread. Mike and Dr. Won were standing near the door, talking with several of the guests. After introducing me to the others, Dr. Won suggested that Mike and I follow him to the buffet line for some breakfast.

The food looked wonderful, not at all what I was accustomed to, but interesting and appealing. There must have been a dozen or more selections of fruit: raw fruit, such as orange, grapefruit, and pineapple, fruit medleys, and even a couple of hot fruit dishes. There were several breads, yogurts, some unusual casseroles, and a couple of dishes unlike any breakfast food I'd seen. But there were no eggs, meats, coffee rolls, no milk products other than yogurt—and there was no coffee.

Dr. Won suggested I try the jiffad, a casserole made with figs, and handed me a cup of tea made from yellow jasmine. The two, he said, would help complete my recovery from the migraine. He said I should consider eliminating citrus fruits, chocolate, and alcohol from my diet.

I wondered if two out of three would be enough. I wasn't ready to give up my Scotch.

When I asked Dr. Won if there was a special significance to the foods being served, he answered that everything at the Center was intended to serve a healing purpose. "The body reacts to both inner and outer stimuli," he said. "By determining what inner stimulus is necessary, we can cause reactions, which aid the healing process."

I picked up the jiffad and a bowl of yogurt with bananas as Dr. Won continued. "All foods have a purpose, not only to fill an empty stomach, but also to assist with the specific needs of the body. When we understand how to use food as medicine, we can strengthen the body's abilities to combat disease and maintain perfect health."

We were directed to a table where several others were already seated. After a brief introduction, Dr. Won continued his discussion.

"For thousands of years man has used certain teas in the treatment of disease," he said. "Yet modern science has ignored the healing properties of such teas, herbs, and foods. Science has only recently begun to rediscover the medicinal value offered by these elements."

He continued. "The body has a built-in mechanism to alert us when we are in need of certain nutrients. That is often the message of cravings. However, many of our present-day cravings are artificially brought about by food addictions that come from an uneducated approach to eating. Food is often selected for taste. Unfortunately, that is influenced by the sugar or fat content, with no regard for the body's actual needs."

Dr. Won spoke to the others at the table explaining our purpose for being there. He asked if they would like to discuss their health problems with us.

Bob, a tall, slender man with bright red hair, was the first to speak. He was seated across from me and looked directly towards me as he spoke. He described how he had been at the Center for a month, receiving treatment for a chronic ulcer problem. "I'm beginning to learn how to listen to my body," he said. "Now that I know what it's saying, I'm better able to control the loss of tissue within my stomach. It is no longer necessary for my body to express its needs through disease. I listen and respond accordingly."

I thought about my experience with the migraine. Dr. Won had instructed me to listen to my body, to discover the message of the headache; and something had rid me of the pain. But the answer, I felt, had to be more complex. It couldn't be that simple.

Bob sipped his tea and continued, "On another and more significant level, I'm learning to listen to my mind through meditation. I am more than my body and more than my thoughts, connected with everything in my experience. Through an expansion of consciousness, I've learned how to control my illness and, more importantly, how to control the direction of my life. But my words can't describe what the Center has meant to me. You have to experience it. The interesting thing is: everyone's experience is different, sometimes dramatically different."

While he was speaking, Bob had never looked away, directing his attention towards me. Instead of making me uncomfortable, however, his gaze and facial expression connected me with his story, and I sensed his sincerity, his total belief in the treatment he'd received. When he finished, he gave a broad smile and looked towards the others at the table. They all nodded.

One by one, each told their story, describing their illnesses and experiences. They seemed to be in agreement that the Center had provided them with the means to overcome disease and had shown them new ways of expression and understanding.

I remained at the table long after completing breakfast, listening to the accounts of those around me. Their stories were interesting, convincing me that the Center was producing positive results. However, I was not at all sure how or why their system worked and wondered if I would be able to translate the experiences into a format that would accomplish our goals.

As we left the dining hall, Dr. Won ask if I would like to accompany him on his morning rounds. He said he liked to monitor each patient's progress and regularly offer positive feedback.

"It is important," he said, "to let each guest know you do not condemn them because of their limitations. Our purpose is to show how such limitations can be overcome. We teach our guests to be aware of their inner resources. Such understanding helps them conquer disease and deal with other problems as well, both within and without the body.

"I will introduce you to Ellen," he said, pointing to a door leading to what he described as the *centering room*. "This room is used to contact the higher self. All new guests spend at least three hours each day in exercises designed to quiet the mind. With our guidance they learn how to meditate and draw upon their healing abilities."

We entered the room, a large open area with dozens of straw mats covering the floor. A small group was meditating at the rear. In the far corner, away from the others, I saw Paula. She seemed to be in deep meditation. I wondered what messages she was receiving.

We followed Dr. Won across the room, where a woman, who appeared to be in her late thirties, sat cross-legged on one of the mats. She looked up as we approached.

"Good morning Ellen," Dr. Won spoke in a whisper. "I would like you to meet Dan Murphy. Dan is here with Dr. West who, I believe, you met on your last visit. Dan and Dr. West are writing a book about our methods of treatment. Would you like to tell them about your experiences at the Center?"

Ellen stood and shook my hand. "Welcome to the Center, Dan." She turned to Mike. "It's nice to see you again, Dr. West. I was just completing my meditation. Perhaps we should go outside."

Ellen led us out a sliding glass door that opened onto the courtyard I'd seen the day before. We walked over to the wooden benches that encircled the pond and sat down.

"What can I tell you that would be helpful?" she asked.

Mike remained silent so I answered. "I'd like to know about your illness. How was it diagnosed, and what led you to the Center?"

"To begin with," she said. "I've been coming to the Center for about four years, spending two weeks each spring and fall, although my initial visit lasted almost three months."

"I would think," I said, "that the average individual would find that difficult, if not impossible, both from a financial standpoint as well as a personal one—especially if one had a family."

"If you're asking if I'm financially independent, the answer is no, not from a traditional viewpoint. However, I believe one can find the resources to accomplish anything, if the need is genuine and the desire is strong.

"The Center is less expensive than you might imagine and has provided much more than a mere physical cure. Because of the costs, I couldn't have continued with standard medical treatment, and it wasn't helping much anyway. Here, I have found the ability to cope with my illness, should it reoccur, and have developed new insights that will, I hope, keep me disease free for the remainder of my life."

"Please excuse me," Dr. Won interrupted. "I must attend to my duties. When you are finished here, have someone page me and we will continue our discussion."

I thanked Dr. Won for his assistance, and he hurried back into the building. I still wanted to quiz him about my experience with the migraine, but I could wait. I needed time to think about the questions I would ask.

"Now, where were we?" Ellen asked. "Oh yes, I was telling you how I discovered the Center. I came here on the recommendation of a friend. I have lupus; well, at least I used to have it. I'd been receiving conventional medical treatment for about three years without any improvement in my condition and, in fact, seemed to be experiencing a continual state of decline.

"It was only by coincidence—of course Dr. Won says there is no such thing as coincidence—that I even discovered the Center. I was returning from a shopping trip with three of my friends when we heard one of those public service announcements about breast examinations on the radio. One of my friends commented on the need for regular medical check ups, that a routine visit to her doctor had detected breast cancer several years earlier. The progression of her disease, she said, was pretty rapid and the treatment seemed ineffective. On the recommendation of a friend, and with the approval of her physician, she came here. Her doctor, it seems, was familiar with Dr. Won's work and had referred patients here in the past. Why he hadn't suggested the Center to her earlier, I don't know."

"I'm surprised that a doctor would recommend such a radical approach," I said. "No offense, Mike, but most physicians seem very slow to accept anything that is not grounded in science. I always assumed the medical profession considered practitioners such as Dr. Won to be quacks."

Mike responded, "You'd be surprised at the number of physicians who quietly support facilities such as this. Generally, you don't hear about these doctors, because they're afraid of creating problems for themselves within the medical community. Occasionally, those I would call enlightened, refer severe cases, or cases where allopathic medicine is ineffective, to alternative practitioners."

"Yes," Ellen continued. "My friend said she came to the Center in complete despair, more as an escape from reality than from any belief she might be cured. But a cure is exactly what she received. Her disease went into remission and has remained so for more than eight years. She's convinced the Center is totally responsible.

"A few days after our discussion in her car, I called my friend to find out about this mysterious Center. My friend knew I was not in great shape, though I'd never discussed my disease with her, so I quizzed her and told her about my problem. She told me how her stay at the Center had helped rid her body of disease, but more importantly, had shown her how to gain control of her body and her emotions. And that, she said, had given her the power to deal with whatever might occur in the future."

Ellen looked at me to see how I was reacting to her story. "Believe me," she said. "I had doubts, too. But my friend seemed to have such a positive attitude towards the Center and was convinced her disease had disappeared because of her stay here, I agreed to come and try to defeat the disease that had been destroying my body."

I looked into the pond and reached down, lightly touching the surface. Another anecdote, I thought. How could I make it compelling and get the message to a large audience? My fingers created ripples that spread across the pond—one touch that became many. Maybe that was it. If the book could touch a few, perhaps they would provide the means to spread the message to others. It might work.

Ellen had watched my movements with interest. I looked up at her. She was different from the others I'd met, calm and poised, with a clear vision of her purpose. Something about her reminded me of Paula. She reached out and grasped my hand. "Yes, like the ripples on the water," she said. "You can do it and you will."

I jerked my hand away. "What?" I said.

She gave a brief smile and looked into the pond.

Mike turned toward me with a puzzled look. "So, Ellen, you say you first came here four years ago?" he asked.

"Yes, I came here a couple of months after learning about the place, and I did find relief from my illness. But, as my friend had told me, getting rid of the disease wasn't the most significant part of my cure. The important thing for me was learning how to deal with present and future problems and how to listen to my body so I might properly respond when illness occurs.

"The experience gave me insights into myself I'd never before considered. I gained understanding and tolerance for the actions of those around me. Most importantly, I feel I have the strength and wisdom to deal with whatever the future holds. By returning to the Center periodically, I have that ability reinforced and work on the development of new and more powerful abilities."

"Such as?" I asked. I was embarrassed about my earlier reaction.

"Well, Dr. Won can probably explain it better than I, but I've developed a keen sense of perception that helps me see when my mind is expressing through my body. I've received some unusual messages that, for me, prove the existence of other dimensions.

"Once, shortly after the death of my father, he appeared to me during my meditation and suggested I use a somewhat obscure herb to aid in my recovery. I followed his recommendation and am convinced that it helped.

"I could go on forever extolling the benefits of the Center, but I'm sure you need to hear from others, too. Can I answer anything else for you?" Ellen stopped speaking, looked at me and smiled. It was the same smile I'd seen on so many of the others.

"No thanks," I said. "Mike and I will catch up with Dr. Won. Thanks for your help."

I wanted to ask her about her "other abilities," as she'd called them, wanted to know how she seemed to have read my thoughts, but I was uncomfortable with the subject. Perhaps I didn't want the answer.

"Thanks for your time," Mike said. "It was a pleasure seeing you again."

We excused ourselves and walked towards the building. Ellen's story was compelling and caused me to question some of my previously held concepts. I'd begun to see how thoughts affect our bodies and how our minds seemed to have far more potential than we imagine. However, her experience was another of those inexplicable mysteries, which, although interesting, is soon forgotten. Could I make it more?

When we caught up with Dr. Won, he invited us to join him in a group session with about fifteen guests. I was amazed with the doctor's awareness of the most obscure and insignificant details of each patient's condition.

There were people in the group with almost every disease imaginable, common illnesses such as heart disease and cancer, and rare and unusual diseases with which I was totally unfamiliar. Each one seemed to accept their illness and their miraculous recovery with the serenity one expects to find in a cult. Though they appeared sincere, I found it difficult to accept everything I'd heard.

Tom, a friend of Ellen's, said he had suffered from severe asthma since childhood, only to have been completely cured during his first day at the Center. He said he regarded illness as a signal that something in him needed to change and welcomed such signals with the understanding that they generated positive results, far exceeding any temporary unpleasantness in his body. Tom seemed eager to report to Dr. Won that he'd been experiencing a digestive problem and had been working in the centering room to discover the message of his problem.

During the next three days, I interviewed more than a dozen others and began to outline the book. I had hoped to spend more time talking with Ellen, but she was at the end of her stay and left the day after we met. However, she did take time to find me and tell me goodbye before leaving.

"I know you have questions," she said. "But many of them you must answer on your own. I look forward to reading your book. I'm sure it will be a success."

Yes, I had many questions, but I hoped she was right. Maybe I would find answers and create success for the book.

After Ellen left I decided to spend time in the centering room. Dr. Won had suggested that I meditate and had shown me a relaxation technique that, he said, would help me reach a meditative state. I spent time each morning and evening working on my meditation. By the end of the week I had developed the basic concept for the book and felt more relaxed than I had in years. I'd even received some brief insights into what I believed to be my real self.

Although I had begun to feel comfortable in the environment and would have enjoyed spending more time at the Center, I needed to return to Boston and begin working on the book. Mike and I had agreed upon a generous division of the profits the book might generate, and he had offered to pay me ten-thousand dollars for the production of the first draft.

I'd finally found some meaningful work and was no longer concerned that the premise seemed a bit far-fetched. There appeared to be enough people who accepted the concept to make it salable, perhaps even lucrative, but somehow it all seemed hollow. I felt curiously restless, discontent.

While the Center had provided a wealth of experiences and information that would become the foundation for the book, the healings, regardless how miraculous they seemed, left me with many unanswered questions. I continually asked why, not why the healings occurred, but why were they necessary? Why did mankind have to experience disease and misfortune? And what about all those kind, loving, and deserving people

70

who never had the opportunity to find a place such as the Center? It didn't seem fair, and the few answers I received were difficult to accept..

Mike and Paula planned to remain in Phoenix for another week, so I returned to Boston alone, excited about a new and different writing assignment. Despite my doubts, I was eager to begin.

CHAPTER 6

PARADIGMS LOST

The flight home was uneventful and I leaned back to enjoy it. Although my stay at the Center had been great, it was nice to get a break and relax for a couple of hours. There would soon be work to do, real work. And for the first time in several years, I felt optimistic.

In the days that followed I continued my research and began the rough draft. Mike had given me his voluminous notes and we spent several hours each week discussing the material he had gathered. I was glad I had a grasp of the fundamentals of medicine—my father had been an orthopedic surgeon and I'd done some pre-med work in school—for a basic understanding of the terminology and methodology was essential.

Although I'd become disillusioned with medicine during my senior year, my limited medical background made it easier for me to find the information I needed and to comprehend that information once I found it.

Mike's notes, combined with my own research, soon filled the small cabin on my boat. It was difficult keeping everything organized and my table became a cluttered jumble of papers. My financial condition, however, made finding more spacious conditions out of the question, so I was elated when Mike suggested I move into his guesthouse at the beach.

"Would it be terribly inconvenient for you to move up here while we work on the book?" Mike asked. "I think it would be helpful and would facilitate our exchange of information."

"Yes," I said, trying to contain my excitement. "It probably would make things a bit easier."

In less than a week I had moved in. The environment stimulated my ability to write and the quiet evenings provided an opportunity for reflection and meditation. I was in heaven and wrote with the intensity and determination I'd experienced four years earlier.

The beach offered comfort to my troubled soul and I could lose myself in the multi-faceted beauty of the surrounding forest. I spent hours acquainting myself with its many trails, saturating my senses in the sights and sounds of nature. The musty smell of damp leaves mixed with the freshness of new pine brought back memories, sometimes painful, that returned me to a time and place I'd tried to erase from memory.

In my mind's eye, I saw Susan sitting on the rocks at sunset, her hair tossed by a spring breeze, and I felt sadness for what might have been.

But I could never retrace those steps. I had a new life. I wished she could see me. Maybe she could understand; maybe she would forgive.

My writing flowed without effort as I worked in the quiet serenity surrounding me, and I soon developed the structure of the book. I enjoyed working on a project with purpose, with meaning, and yet, there was still a void. Something was missing. I needed some unidentifiable bit of information in order to pull everything together and decided to discuss the problem with Mike. He seemed to understand and suggested I accompany him to the Philippines.

"I have a friend in Manila," he said. "Perhaps he can provide you with some answers. I haven't seen him in several months and I could use some of his wisdom myself."

The next day Mike made arrangements for our trip and we left the following Monday. Paula was in San Francisco visiting her father and did not join us.

****

At the Manila airport, Mike's friend, Mario, literally greeted us with open arms. "Welcome to my little country," he said as he gave me a bear hug. His huge arms encircled my body, pinning my hands to my side. Unaccustomed to greeting strangers with such enthusiasm, I felt uncomfortable and pulled away as soon as he released his grasp.

"You are Dan," Mario said. He spoke with only a slight accent. "Mike has told me you want to learn about our healing techniques. That is good. We have healing methods that have been passed down through many generations, and I am sure you are familiar with our famous psychic surgery."

Mario's voice boomed from a massive frame. Although I wouldn't describe him as overweight, I guessed him to be forty to fifty pounds heavier than I, yet no more than an inch or so taller. His dark complexion, hair, and eyes made him appear somewhat mysterious, but his jovial attitude quickly dispelled such a notion. I was captivated by his wit and charm.

"Yes," Mike said. "I would like for Dan to see some examples of your healing methods. But, more importantly, we both need to discuss some problems we have in understanding how it all fits together. We recently spent some time at a healing center in the United States and need some clarification of the mind-body relationship for a book we're writing."

"That is not necessarily and easy task," Mario answered. He began to load our luggage into his car. "Some things, once seen, may be easy to acknowledge, but difficult for the mind to process. Our minds are finite and are accustomed to dealing with things that can be quantified, but healing involves the infinite and understanding is limited. Perhaps I can be of assistance. I will think about what you ask."

We drove north from the airport through an area Mario said was called, Makati. I was impressed by the expressways, modern buildings, and the sophisticated atmosphere.

"This is not at all as I envisioned," I said. "This reminds me of New York."

"This is only a small part of Manila," Mario said. He chuckled. "You may also see the part which fits your expectation. Manila is a city of many cities, several of which were combined to form Metro Manila. It is also a city of contrasts. We have the elite financial centers you see here as well as some of the worst slums in the world, which you will also see."

We continued through Makati and crossed the Pasig River, which splits Manila into two very distinct parts. The opposite shore provided a view of the city, dramatically different from the first. The area was much poorer and more congested. This, I thought, was more like I had pictured.

Mario seemed to have read my thoughts. "Now, you see a different side of Manila. This is the Filipino side. The other side is—if you will pardon the expression —too Americanized for me.

"Let me show you something," he said. He steered the car down a narrow street and stopped next to an iron gate. "This is the Chinese Cemetery, a city for the dead."

The place was incredible, unlike anything I'd ever seen. It looked more like a small village than a cemetery, complete with streets and houses.

"Many of these houses," Mario said, "have electricity, running water, air conditioning and are much better than we poor Filipinos can afford. The families of the deceased frequently come to visit their dead relatives, bring gifts, and even play games with them. Although," Mario paused and laughed. "I think it is not difficult to win at games in here."

As he led us down the narrow streets of the cemetery, I marveled at the attention to detail. There was ornate stained glass, expensive ironwork, and even mailboxes for the dead. It was obvious that many were concerned that their dead relatives might be participating in life on some level.

Mario stopped in front of one particularly elaborate burial mansion. "You want to understand the connection between the mind and the body," he said. "Look at this house. The body of some wealthy Chinese is here. Do you think he occupies this home in the same fashion he did his residence, prior to his death?

"The body is here," he continued. "But is the intelligence? In the same manner, you believe your mind occupies your physical body. Is that

76

possible? Think about that for a moment. Can you tell me the location of your mind?

"The mind is a process, not something that can be located with tests and expensive equipment. Your mind is, in fact, located both within and without your body. It is your body and everything in your experience."

"Hold on," I said. "You're getting into unexplored territory. What you say sounds interesting, but it's the stuff philosophers have pondered for centuries. As far as I can tell, you can neither prove nor disprove it. So, what's the purpose?"

"Mike, have you brought me a skeptic to test my powers of persuasion?" Mario asked.

"It's not only Dan," Mike responded. "I need help with this, too. The pure healing part I understand, learning to focus the brain and getting it to generate the chemicals necessary to cure an illness. What I don't understand is absentee healing, the healing of an infant, and how we can still be so inconsistent with our results."

Mario looked at us as a broad grin spread across his dark-skinned face. "You have come here to find answers to your questions. Yes, I may give you some answers, but I think you will leave with more questions than you brought. Truth is not so easy to define, and Spirit may have some lessons for all of us. We must keep our eyes and our hearts open and be ready to seize the opportunities for enlightenment when they arise. Now, we must hurry to my home. The rain will soon come."

Though Mario may have been enigmatic with his answers, he was certainly correct about the rain. It was staggering. I've never seen so much water fall in such a short time. The rainy season, Mario explained, had just begun, and street flooding sometimes created dangerous situations.

Mario's house was located in an area called Tondo, an overcrowded slum that reminded me of the poverty I'd seen in Mexico City. Although his neighborhood was obviously poor, the area adjacent to his house was amazingly clean and well maintained. His front yard was filled with flowers and perfectly manicured.

"I live here," Mario said. His voice and facial expression displayed obvious pride. "I have remained in this neighborhood for many reasons. It helps my poor countrymen identify with me and trust that I have their interests at heart. I do my healing work here.

"Come," he said. "I will show you something." He pointed to a small vegetable garden at the rear of his house.

As we stood under the roof of a narrow covered porch, Mario gestured toward the garden. "Look," he said. "That tomato plant is suffering from disease while its twin over here experiences perfect health. Do you think one plant is more blessed or more in harmony with its divine nature than the other?

"No, of course not," he continued. "The diseased plant has simply picked up a contaminate or a parasite from the environment and is suffering the consequences. Spirit or God, as some call It, always allows nature to proceed as planned. The disease is neither good nor bad, but is only an occurrence from which we may learn something.

"In the case of my tomato plant, I may learn that I have not spent enough time or effort with my garden. In the case of a sick child, we, the parents or neighbors, may learn compassion, giving, or the ability to listen. Is the child's suffering unfair? No, and it should not be regarded in a negative fashion. It is all part of a great mystery, a process in which we are allowed to participate."

The rain was coming hard, the water running off Mario's roof in torrents. I noted an elaborate drainage system, however, that channeled the water away from his house and around his garden.

He seemed aware of my interest and said, "This, too, is part of the process. Spirit provides the rain, but it is my responsibility to direct the flow. In the same manner, we are filled with Prana, the energy of life, but we must be open to receive and must direct that energy to our highest purpose. Remember to listen with your heart, to open your mind to the boundless possibilities that exist. Our limited view of life sometimes blinds us to our potential for growth.

"Everyone is divine in nature and express that divinity in many ways. We should not ignore or criticize the condition of someone whose reality we do not share. We must do everything in our power to assist another and should not question the reasons behind their situation."

"This is all very esoteric," I said. "I'm afraid the average person will find your views somewhat difficult to accept. Most people do have a different picture of reality."

"Yes, you are correct," he said, "And I am not a good teacher. If you would like, I will introduce you to someone who may be able to clarify things much better than I."

"Yes," Mike said. "We would like that very much."

"First," Mario said, "I have a some people coming for treatment. You can observe our healing methods. Perhaps that will provide additional insights into your questions."

The rain never slowed, but Mario's patients soon began arriving for treatment. Although there were no scheduled appointments, everyone seemed to arrive at the appropriate time, with practically no waiting between the healing sessions.

"Our doctors could use some pointers on scheduling their patients," Mike said. "I'm amazed by your ability to deal with so many people in such an organized manner."

"That is a function of listening," Mario responded. "I listen and I have shown my friends how to listen also. When we are in harmony with our true nature and with each other, it is natural to express that harmony in all we do."

He stopped speaking as a small boy entered the room. "Hello, Juan," Mario greeted the boy and held out his arms. Come, I want you to meet two of my friends from America."

The boy appeared frightened and moved to Mario's side, hiding most of his frail body behind the protecting legs of the healer. "Tell me," Mario said. He stroked the boy's head. "How are you feeling?" Juan looked up and nodded.

"Do not be afraid," Mario said. "These are friends. This is Dan and Mike. They live in America. Tell them about your illness."

The boy looked up at Mario and his fear seemed to subside. He began speaking in broken English. "I have . . . had problem with eyes. I could not see. Now, I go to school and can read. I learn to speak English and will go to America."

"What was his problem," I asked.

"He was blind, virtually blind," Mario said. "His vision only allowed him to distinguish light from darkness. I have been treating Juan for about two years. Though his vision is not as clear as yours or mine, he is continuing to improve and should be perfect after a few more treatments."

"How do you treat him?" Mike asked.

"I visualize Juan with perfect sight and transfer that vision to him," he answered. As he spoke he placed his hands on the boy's head. "I send my energy, my prana, into the nerves and cells that control his sight. It is like using one car with a strong battery to start another with a weak one. I am simply the mechanism through which Divine Nature flows."

"Why not effect a complete cure in one session? Why has it taken so long to cure him?" I asked.

"I can not answer your question," Mario said. "Spirit shows me what is necessary in each case. Time is irrelevant to Spirit and to me. Each person, each soul, is unique, requiring different times to bring about their cure. Of course, some never receive a cure. But it is not for me to question the methods of Spirit or the needs of another. I am simply honored to participate in the process."

After holding his hands on the boy's head for a few minutes, Mario told him he could go. "Do not forget to study your English," he said.

The boy waved and ran out the door.

I had begun to express my skepticism, when a woman ran into the room with a young boy, his arm bleeding through a towel wrapped around a wound.

"Please help my son," the woman pleaded. "He has fallen into the river and cut his arm on the rocks. Please. Quickly. He is bleeding."

Mario pulled the towel from the boy's arm exposing a nasty gash, about four inches long. The boy appeared to be going into shock as blood squirted out of the cut and pooled on the floor. I thought I saw the flash of bone as Mario placed the arm on his lap.

Holding one hand slightly above the cut, he spoke to the boy. "You must not play in the river when it rains. The current is swift and you may suffer an injury much more serious than a simple cut."

The boy immediately appeared to be more calm. As the color returned to his face, the bleeding stopped.

81

Mario continued to talk to the boy and began a slight stroking motion with his hand held about three inches above the boy's arm. Occasionally, he stopped and appeared to flick some invisible matter from his fingers. After a couple of minutes, he rested his hand directly on the injured area. I could no longer see the cut, but from the look on the boy's face, I knew Mario had somehow relieved both the fear and the pain. We sat in silence. After a span of not more than ten minutes, Mario removed his hand from the boy's arm. I looked on in amazement. The cut had completely closed, and there was only a long red scar, about one-half inch wide. I'd found what I'd come for: a miraculous healing.

The woman thanked Mario at least a dozen times and continued offering thanks as the healer ushered the two out the door. "Remember," he called to the boy. "Stay away from the river when it rains."

I could not wait for them to leave, eager to question Mario about what he had done. "What just happened?" I asked. "How did you do that?"

He turned to me and smiled. "We have been provided with an example of what we discussed and have seen how one body responds to the energy of another. I think you will now agree that such powers exist."

"But," I protested, "Can you explain the mechanism by which this miracle occurred? Seeing it happen is not enough. This perfectly illustrates my confusion about healing. I don't understand."

"What you saw was no miracle," he said. "Our experience was in harmony with natural law. The phenomenon is your inability to accept it. When the rain stops, I will take you to meet my teacher. Perhaps he can further your understanding."

As soon as the rain began to subside, Mario helped us load our things into his car for the trip to meet his teacher. We drove north and he gave us a brief history of the area. "We are going to Pangasinan, where we grow much of our rice. There are many legends about the area. You will also be interested to know that most of our psychic surgery is done in that province."

After driving for a couple of hours, we entered a low flood plain. Huge fields of rice spread before us in all directions. Although we had experienced a brief period of sunshine after leaving Manila, I suspected the improvement to be only temporary, for dark clouds were forming along the hills to our west. As we turned onto a narrow dirt road, the rain began once more, and soon the ditches beside the road were flowing like small streams. The car strained against the driving rain, and I wondered how Mario could see through the walls of water that beat against the windshield.

"We must stop," Mario said. "But first we should cross the river, about ten kilometers ahead. If the rain continues all night, I fear the bridge may wash away."

We continued sliding along what had become little more than a trail through the woods. After about twenty minutes, he stopped the car. "The bridge is ahead." he said. "I must stop and make certain it is safe for us to cross."

If the bridge washes away, I wondered, how will we return? I kept quiet, though, more concerned about the conditions at hand.

I peered out the window and saw a dark figure step from of the dense underbrush. Without explanation Mario got out of the car, and the two held a brief conversation. A moment later he jumped back in.

"The bridge is not safe," he said. "We must wait here until morning."

"Who was that?" Mike asked.

"Eleuterio," he said. "My teacher. He came to warn us about the bridge, but has gone to help a family that has been injured by the flood. He will return in the morning."

"Has he been waiting for us all evening?" I asked. "How did he know we were here?"

"He knows," Mario answered. "You will see."

CHAPTER 7

ELETUERIO

The next morning, I awoke with a start as Mario slammed the car door. "Sorry, my friends. Did I wake you?"

"No problem," I said. I pushed the seat forward and opened the door. My back and legs ached, and when I stood, I almost fell.

"It is a good day." Mario said. "No rain. How was your sleep?"

"Not the best," I said. My boat was not much, but it was the Ritz compared to Mario's car. And the noise—Jesus! I thought the occasional bumping of the hull against the pilings was annoying, but Mario's snoring was incredible.

Mike agreed. "I love camping," he said. "But I like my tent better."

I looked at the surrounding hills, obscured in rain and darkness the previous night. The area was thick with low-growing vegetation with few tall, slender trees punctuating the dense covering, rising high above the forest floor.

Mario retrieved a bundle from his car and invited us to join him for breakfast. "Here," he said, opening his package. "I brought food for us. As you can see," He patted his stomach. "I do not like to miss my meals."

As he spoke, a shrill cry came from the forest, instantly bringing back memories of my ordeal at sea, months earlier. The sound was the same as I'd heard from the strange bird that had circled my boat.

"What was that?" I asked.

"A bird, perhaps," Mario responded. "I do not spend much time in the forest. I am not familiar with the cries of the birds and animals."

The call sounded again. There was no doubt. It was the same as I'd heard on Conquest and gave me an uneasy feeling.

Whatever had made the sound never appeared, and I looked toward Mario as he began to speak. "Please join me for breakfast," he said. He pointed to the food. "I apologize for not providing better sustenance; there was little time to prepare."

Our breakfast consisted of a few slices of hard bread and a wedge of cheese that Mario divided into three pieces. He also produced two bright yellow fruit, which he began to peel. "Mango," he said. "The real fruit of the gods." He appeared to give a silent blessing and instructed us to eat.

The bread was hard and rather bland, but the cheese was strong and flavorful. And the mango—delicious. The food tasted as good as any breakfast at Walden's.

As we finished our meal, I looked up to see Mario's friend coming down the road. "Hello Mario," he called. "It is good that you did not try to cross the bridge. It has washed away during the night."

Mario's friend wore a large floppy hat that shadowed his face, but I could see his teeth gleaming in a broad smile. He walked over to Mario and hugged him warmly. "How are you, my friend?" he asked. "It pleases me to see you. And who have you brought to our humble province ?"

"These are my friends from America. This is Mike, the American doctor I told you about, and this," Mario pointed to me. "This is Dan who asks many questions about our healing methods."

"I am Eleuterio," he said, extending his hand to me. "But you may call me Lou."

As I reached to grasp his hand, I saw his face for the first time. I froze, unable to move or speak. I felt I'd stepped into a surreal dream world, detached from what was happening around me. As I observed the scene, terror gripped my mind.

The face—the eyes—yes, those dark, piercing eyes. I recognized him immediately as the stranger I'd encountered at sea! But how could that be? How could he have been there? I remembered the article about Paula West.

My heart pounded and I was certain everyone could hear it. I could feel every drop of blood pulsating through my veins, every molecule of air entering my lungs.

Somewhere in the distance, I heard Mike's voice. "Dan, are you okay? You look ill."

My mind formed the words to respond, but I couldn't speak. I was disoriented. Everything was moving.

My knees buckled, and the stranger reached out with powerful hands and grabbed me. I sensed his strength as one hand slipped under my arm and kept me from falling. He eased me to the ground, and I slouched against the boulder we had earlier used as a table. He stood over me without speaking.

I was conscious of everything, yet unable to move or speak. I was certain I'd had a stroke—there in the godforsaken jungle, no medical facilities I would trust. I was going to die.

Mario and the stranger stepped near the car and began talking. Maybe I was already dead, I thought. But I could hear them. I heard enough of their conversation to know they were talking about me.

Mike checked my pulse, trying to determine what was wrong. I could sense his concern. He backed away when the stranger approached.

With one hand on the back of my neck, the stranger placed a cup to my lips. "Drink," he said. "This is my cure for seeing ghosts."

Mario bellowed with laughter. I couldn't believe they were treating my condition so lightly. It was obvious they didn't realize the seriousness of the situation.

"Drink," the stranger said again. He tilted the cup. "This is a special mixture."

I spread my lips and allowed the liquid flow into my mouth. It smelled like rotten eggs and tasted worse. I choked and sprayed the stranger with the foul-smelling brew.

Once more Mario roared with laughter.

"I think he is alive," the stranger said.

"I don't think he likes your tea," Mario responded.

Mike stepped near me. "Are you okay?" he asked.

I gasped for breath. "You . . . you're not going to believe this," I said, finally able to speak. "I don't believe it myself. But I've seen this guy before . . . near Boston . . . on my boat. He fixed my engine."

Both Mario and the stranger had overheard what I said and howled with laughter. Mike didn't seem to share their sense of humor and gripped my shoulder. "That doesn't make sense," he said. "Mario's friend may look like some mechanic you met, but he couldn't be the same person."

"You don't understand," I said. "I know it's crazy, but I saw him a few months ago. He came to my boat and left a magazine article about healing—about Paula's healing."

"You're right," Mike said. "It sounds crazy, but I'm convinced you believe what you're saying."

"Is it not amazing the workings of Spirit?" Mario interrupted, "You have received a gift, an opportunity for your growth. When you are ready to acknowledge that there is more to life than you see, you will have many experiences that cannot be explained by your rational mind. A new reality has opened before you, a unique and personal reality that others may be unable to share. Allow your awareness to expand and you may soon discover additional steps to take."

"But I saw you, El . . . Eleuterio," I said. "I didn't have a vision."

"Call me Lou," he said. "You will find it much easier."

"Okay, Lou. But we have met and you know it. It was real."

"What is real?" he asked. "Can you describe it for me?"

"Real is something I can feel, something I can touch and hold. Real is the article you left on my boat."

"Ah, so if you can touch it, then it is real?" Lou asked. "And the thing you say I left with you, can you show it to me?"

"Well, I had it, a magazine article, but I must have lost it. The thing was in my coat pocket when I flew to Phoenix, but I couldn't find it afterwards. It was no dream. I held it."

"No," Lou said. "You experienced it. That is what makes it real for you. You believe in the things of your experience. That is the basis of your reality."

"But others," Mario added, "may not share your reality and may experience something you find unacceptable. How is it possible to determine which is more real?"

"Many thousands of your people," Lou continued, "have begun to experience what they call 'fire-walking.' There are those in your country who teach the control of the mind and who conclude their program by having the participants walk across hot coals.

"I find it humorous that those who present such courses seem to believe they have made a great discovery, that the ability of the mind to control or deceive the body is something new. But we, and millions of others across the world and throughout time, have known about and utilized such powers for centuries."

Lou ignored my obvious discomfort and continued. "According to your reality, the hot coals are real. Their temperature can be measured. A physician will tell you that contact with the skin will call severe burns. His conditioning, his training tells him so. However, the participants believe they will not suffer burns, and therefore, they do not. The reality for them is quite different."

"This is crazy," I said. "I don't understand what's happening."

"You will," Lou said. "When you cease denying the existence of those things you cannot comprehend. Now, we must go. Sometimes there are bandits in these hills."

I was dazed and staggered towards the car. I wanted to ask questions, but my mind wouldn't function, unable to translate the incident into any sort of logical or coherent thought process.

Lou grabbed my arm. "We will not take the automobile. The bridge is out. We must walk."

"Will we need our things?" Mike asked.

"No," Lou answered. "You cannot carry anything. The trail is steep and very dangerous."

Great, I thought, Lou saved our lives last night so we can die on some jungle trail. "Where are we going?" I asked.

"We will go to my house," Lou said. "You must not talk. There may be bandits nearby."

As we started into the thick brush, I asked, "Aren't you going to lock the car? I have my camera and my clothes."

"No," Mario answered. "If we lock the car, we draw attention and invite thieves. We must give the appearance that we have nothing of value, that we are not concerned. After all, if thieves come and see the doors locked, do you not think they will break the window?"

Lou paused and turned to me. "Release your attachment to things," he said. "You cannot fully experience the bounty of life if your energy is focused upon possessions. You must LET GO."

Lou led the way through the dense growth of the forest. Though there was almost no trail, he hurried along, silently waving us on as we climbed over fallen trees and boulders that blocked our path.

The trail grew increasingly difficult, and I was amazed at how Lou managed to move so quickly. Though he appeared to be in his sixties, he crawled across giant boulders and up steep embankments without effort. I struggled to keep up. "He must take vitamins," I whispered to myself.

"Do not talk," Lou barked. He never looked back.

After a couple of hours of the most difficult hiking I've ever experienced, we entered a clearing. I could see a house—I suppose it could be called a house—tucked into the trees at the far side. The place looked deserted with large bushes growing through openings in the porch where flooring had once been.

"Welcome to my home," Lou said. He gestured toward the dwelling. "Come in. You will rest while I prepare food."

The house, or shack, as it should more appropriately be called, was no more than twenty feet square and consisted of only one room. As we entered, I noticed a cot, a makeshift cupboard, and a table with two chairs. As far as furnishings went, that was it. But the room was cluttered with boxes of all shapes and sizes and there were a couple of empty wooden crates. The thing I found most interesting, however, was a map, yellow and curled with age and spread across the table, a coastal map of New England.

"What's this?" I asked. I pointed to the map. "Are you planning a trip to America?"

Lou ignored my question, but I wasn't about to let it drop. "You know I'm from Boston, don't you?" I asked. "And you've been to Boston. I saw you."

Lou turned to me. "Yes, I have been to Boston."

"I knew it," I said. "I did see you, didn't I?"

"How could that be?" he said. "My visit to Boston was many years ago, at the end of the war. After the devastation of our country, I lived with relatives in New York for a few years. I returned to my country when you were only a child. I have not been away since."

"That's impossible," I said. "I saw you last March. I know it was you."

"Perhaps you are confused. Almost half a century has passed since I have been away from my poor country."

Mike was obviously embarrassed by the entire exchange and spoke up. "Maybe it was someone who looked like Lou. He said he wasn't in Boston. Couldn't it have been someone else?"

"You don't understand," I said. "None of you do." As I heard myself speaking, I thought how paranoid I sounded, yet I continued trying to convince Mike—convince myself—that I was sane, that what I described had really happened.

"This was not something I dreamed. I know what I saw. It was him. It's all too strange. Explain the map."

"It doesn't matter," Mike whispered. "Forget it."

"If you must know," Lou said. "I discovered the map in some things I had kept from my days in America. I heard about the recent storm that damaged your northeast coast, and I looked at my map to help me understand how near the destruction was to my friends and family"

What Lou said was true. The storm I'd experienced on Conquest had done a lot of damage all along the coast, but that didn't explain how I'd seen him. However, it had become obvious I wasn't going to learn more. In an effort to save face with Mike, I dropped the issue.

"I'm sorry," I said. "I suppose I'm just tired from our trip. So, why didn't you stay in America—after the war, I mean."

"I longed to return to the beauty of my country," Lou answered. He turned to face me. "I missed our mountains, valleys, and our wonderful forests, but most of all, I returned to be with the gentle people of my country. I was not comfortable with the superficial way in which Americans lived their lives. There was so much attachment to things and so little concern for friends and family. I longed for the simple life of the Filipinos."

Mike, who had been uncomfortable during my questioning, looked towards Lou, "Mario tells me that you taught him your healing methods. We would like to understand more about healing and about the specific ways you treat illness."

Mario responded to Mike's question, "Yes, Lou has been my teacher for many years, and he has taught others, too. It is not like your medical school. We learn the ancient ways of healing, but we also learn about ourselves. That teaches us how we can help others."

"After our meal," Lou said, "I will take you to a village that is nearby. Some of our friends were injured by the flood. You can observe our healing methods."

I hoped it was nearby, and that the trail was better than the one we used getting to Lou's.

Mario followed Lou outside and the two began gathering fruit from an area behind the house. As they walked away, I thought I heard my name. I was sure I was the topic of their conversation.

"Mike," I whispered. "I know it sounds crazy, but I saw Lou in Boston. I talked with him. I don't know why he doesn't want us to know, but I think it's a little weird. Don't you?"

"Look," Mike said. "Couldn't you be mistaken? Why would he lie? From the looks of things around here, I doubt he could afford the airfare. Anyway, what difference does it make to our project?"

"I don't know. But I'm not mistaken. I'll find out before we leave."

Lou and Mario stepped back into the room carrying several fruit, which they placed on the table. "We will eat before our next journey," Lou said.

I recognized papaya and mango, but there were a couple of varieties with which I was totally unfamiliar. Lou peeled and sliced them all, placing the pieces into a large bowl before us. I reached to take a slice, but Lou stopped me.

"Wait. We must give thanks and prepare the food for our bodies."

Lou placed a large jar that appeared to be filled with water, next to the fruit. He held out his hands, palms downward, over the food.

"Thank you Spirit," he began, "for this food. Send your healing, cleansing light that we may be filled with energy, with prana, for health, for nourishment and enlightenment. We give thanks and it is done."

Lou stepped back and gestured toward the food. "Now eat," he said.

The fruit was great, except for one type that had an unusual and somewhat bitter taste. Lou noticed that I'd avoided it after an initial sampling. He insisted I eat my portion.

"Spirit has provided our food and has filled it with prana. You must eat in order to absorb the energy into your body."

I ate the remaining fruit, then Lou passed around the water jar. "Drink well. It is time to go."

The hike to the village was much easier than our first and we arrived in about an hour. The village consisted of only five houses, all located within a small clearing at the edge of a creek. The houses were almost identical—no windows, unpainted wood siding, and rusting metal roofs.

On the way over, Lou explained that when the storm hit, one of the families had been returning from a visit to relatives who lived nearby. The villagers were crossing a makeshift bridge when it collapsed, spilling everyone into the swollen creek.

95

The father was able to reach the shore, but was unable to rescue his wife and two small children who were clinging to the branches of a partially submerged tree. The man rushed into the village and, with the help of his neighbors, pulled his family to safety. However, the wife and children had suffered some severe cuts and bruises, and one child had a broken arm.

Lou explained how he had treated the family the previous night, relieved their pain, and had given them herbs to help them rest. "But several treatments will be required for proper healing," he said.

He motioned for us to follow him into one of the houses. Inside, we found the family resting on straw mats. One of the villagers, an older woman dressed in a simple cloth wrap, was feeding the children. Lou spoke to her briefly and then stepped near the two adults. Gesturing towards them, he said, "This is Andres' and his wife, Anita. I have explained to them that you are my students and are here to learn the Filipino way of healing. They have agreed to let me show you how Spirit heals their wounds."

The healer knelt near Anita and spoke softly. "Before I begin the healing process, I examine the energy field to get a view of the area in need of healing." He held his hands about a foot from the woman and slowly moved them from her head to her feet.

"The prana tells me if there is a disturbance in the body. In this case, much was obvious because their wounds were visible. However, Anita had internal damage that was not visible and, of which, she was unaware."

Lou clasped Anita's tiny hands in his. She looked up at him, her small body trembling. Within seconds she seemed to relax, and her chest moved with slow, deep breaths.

"I'm familiar with the body's energy field," I said. "But how do you remedy a disturbance, as you call it, and how does that affect the physical body?"

"We are beings of vibration," he answered. "All of us can see the physical body because it vibrates at a much lower level than does the non-physical or pranic body. But there are many who also see the other body. Anyone can be trained to see the energy and can learn to manipulate it to assist in healing.

"See this scar," Lou said. He moved to Andres' and lifted the man's arm. "Yesterday, this was an open cut and the prana was depleted. Today, it is closed, and Andres' feels no discomfort. I applied a salve of ground kamote leaves to help with the healing and then transferred my energy to his arm in order to re-supply Andres' prana.

"It is not difficult to feel the pranic flow around the body," he continued. "Once that is understood, then learning how to heal the body by manipulating the prana is also easy."

Lou moved to one of the children. "This child had a broken arm," he said. "The break caused a hole in the prana. I closed the hole and used my hands to send energy into the arm to generate healing vibrations."

Lou spent more time with Anita and with the other child, talking to them and passing his hands a few inches above their bodies. When he had finished, he thanked them for allowing us to witness their treatment. He stood and turned to Mike and me.

"You have seen how we use the body's energy field to assist in healing, and you can write about what you have seen. The healing you have witnessed, however, is only a small and insignificant part of our work. There are many steps beyond healing where it is possible to reach a state of consciousness allowing one to transcend the body, a state where illness does not exist. When you are ready to learn and experience such a state, a teacher will appear."

My mind was in overload. I'd experienced things far beyond my expectations, things, which, if described in my normal life, would make me a candidate for some serious therapy. I was eager to return to civilization and attempt to translate my experiences into a form that would make them acceptable to both an eager public and a skeptical medical profession. I was pleased when Lou announced that we must return to his home.

After expressing our thanks to Andres' and his family, we left for the walk back to Lou's. As we walked, Mario spoke. "I hope the demonstration has been beneficial, but our healings were not done to impress you. Our efforts are intended to draw attention to what is becoming a lost art. Very few in the modern world accept the things you have witnessed today. Our wish is that by sharing this knowledge we may preserve it for future generations.

"Man has stepped near the edge of the precipice. A few steps more and he may be lost, but a few steps toward a connection with his lost heritage may bring about a state of being that cannot be imagined. I do not know which steps man will take."

We walked the trail in silence. I contemplated the implications of what we had seen.

When we reached Lou's house, we rested for a time and Lou announced he would be unable to stay with us, that he needed to check on a friend who lived alone, a half-day's walk into the mountains. I reminded him that it would soon be dark, but he apologized and said he could not wait until morning. He would leave immediately.

"You are welcome to stay the night in my home," he said. "And I wish you good journey for I will not return for many days. Remember," he said, his dark, piercing eyes looking directly into mine, "Healing is only the beginning. There is much more for you to do." He paused and grasped my hand. "And for you, there is much more to learn." He turned and walked away, disappearing into the shadows.

I might have protested, might have asked him to explain, but I hadn't recovered from our meeting the day before. At the moment I had no more questions, and if I had, I wasn't sure I would have wanted the answers. I was ready to go home.

The next day, Mario led us back to his car, which, I noted, had not been disturbed. After some difficulty in turning the car around, we were soon bouncing along the road that led down the mountain. I looked out the rear window as the morning sun climbed above the jagged peaks behind us. The bright light glistened on the lush growth of the forest, and I marveled at the dramatic shift in weather conditions from two days earlier.

I appreciated the absence of rain and watched as the area we had driven through passed by. The morning light revealed a view of the road that had been obscured in darkness only two nights before. Though the scenery was beautiful, the road was treacherous, with deep ruts, precarious turns, and steep cliffs all around. I was amazed we had made it as far as we had and thankful to have survived.

Mike sat up front with Mario, discussing the specifics of some of the healing techniques and making notes about the herbal medicines used by the healers. However, I was overwhelmed by what I'd seen. I tried to push some of the more bizarre experiences from my mind. I thought about the book and began to expand my strategy for its development. It had become clear that success was within my grasp, and I was determined to reach it.

Back in Manila, Mike and I expressed our sincere thanks and said goodbye to Mario. "It is I who owes a debt of gratitude," he responded, embracing us warmly. "You have provided an opportunity to share our knowledge and preserve it for the future. I thank you and I give thanks to Spirit for our time together."

As he left us at the airport, I wished I could experience some of the calmness, the wisdom that both he and Lou exhibited. They seemed content with their place in the universe, a feeling I longed to share.

CHAPTER 8

THE GATHERING STORM

The trip to the Philippines was a blur, filled with insights into how the mind and body are interrelated. I had seen additional cases of so-called spiritual healing, although I felt "spiritual" was not the correct terminology, and had become convinced of the existence of healing forces with which I had little or no understanding. Through some unseen force, the mind appeared capable of curing many of the afflictions plaguing mankind.

In the following weeks I lost myself in my work. Soon after our return from the Philippines, Mike and Paula had taken a trip to North Dakota. Mike had heard of the work being performed by a Native American shaman and was eager to examine the results firsthand.

By the time they returned, I'd completed a rough draft and had begun making corrections. Mike was finalizing the plans for his first alternative healing center, and though we were both progressing toward our goals, portions of the book troubled me. I'd done an adequate job, I thought, of describing cases of non-medical healing and felt the book presented a good argument for alternative healing methods, but something was lacking. There was too much inconsistency in the results that were achieved, and I had no idea how to resolve my confusion. I needed direction, but didn't know how or where to look. The problem was, I wasn't certain what I was seeking. I remembered something Lou had said a few weeks earlier.

"You have everything you need. The answers to your questions can be found within. You are searching for something outside of yourself. That is why you cannot see it. There is nothing separate from you."

I didn't understand what he had meant. And what was it he said about there being much more than healing, and that a teacher would appear when I was ready? It was evident to me that I had come far beyond the ghost writing job I'd envisioned, and the experience had become more fascinating than my wildest fantasy. If only I could understand what I'd seen. If only I could make a connection that would help me see how the healings fit within the framework of my experience.

Healing seemed to be one part of a process, a much larger process, but I had no grasp of what that larger something was. Perhaps I could resolve my questions as they related to the book, but I needed to have a better understanding of how it all worked. And, I thought, maybe the readers

102

would be as confused as I was. The most critical piece of the puzzle seemed to be missing, and if I didn't find it, I feared our book might appear as hollow as the others I'd read.

Though I made progress, I struggled with my uncertainty for several days. Mike was preoccupied with preparations for his healing center and had little time to discuss my problems with me. As far as he was concerned, the book was almost finished.

"Don't be such a perfectionist," he said. "You've already accomplished more than I imagined possible. If we promote the book properly, it will be a success."

However, I was unable to accept my work as complete, and I knew it wouldn't be the end of my study. I felt I'd only begun. My experiences in Phoenix and, more especially, in the Philippines had whetted my appetite for more—more experiences and more understanding. Though I might never find answers and might not comprehend the answers I found, I had to try. It was my nature.

There was but one option. I would return to the Philippines and spend more time with Lou. Maybe he could resolve my dilemma and help me put things in perspective.

Mike was disturbed by my need to leave before finishing the book, and I knew I'd never make him understand. He had problems of his own and had neither the time nor the inclination to deal with mine.

"I know you want to see more," he said. "I do, too. But I need you here. You'll have plenty of time later. Getting the book published is the most critical issue at the moment. You'll have the rest of your life to continue your search, but the time for the book is now. We can't waste this opportunity."

"I'll only be gone a few days," I said. "I'll pay for the trip. I assure you the book will be completed soon and will be even better than it is now. I'm sorry you can't understand my position. It's not something I want to do. I have to go."

Later that day I called the airline and booked a flight for the following Friday. Though Mike didn't understand my reasons for leaving, he contacted Mario, asking him to meet me at the airport. Once the plans were made, however, I was apprehensive, unsure if I was taking the right step, wondering if I would find answers in the Philippines.

I felt like a medieval crusader, obsessed in a search for the Grail, yet doubtful of its true existence. I needed to understand what was happening. Though my belief system had been transformed, I questioned whether or not I'd chosen the right path. I also pondered the somewhat far-fetched possibility that I had not made the choice at all, that the strange path upon which I had embarked had been chosen for me, but if so, by whom or what?

One part of me wished I'd never heard of Mike West, and yet something, much stronger than simple curiosity, kept calling me into a deeper involvement with a mysterious and unexplored world. I was both frightened and aroused by the incredible circumstances surrounding me.

There was a strangely religious or spiritual feeling that pervaded both my questions and the answers I felt—or hoped—would be forthcoming. Though I'd never been a religious person, I felt there was a spiritual discovery to be made. I would soon find out.

Manila appeared the same as it had when I left a few weeks earlier—gray, hot, and raining. Mario met me at the airport and was his usual, jovial self. He greeted me with a smile.

"Why did you return so soon?" he asked. "Did you miss our daily rains?"

"I need to see Lou," I said. "I have some unanswered questions that I feel he can help me with. Can you take me to see him?"

"I'm afraid that may not be an easy task," Mario said. "The rain has continued since you left, and many roads and bridges have been damaged."

"I must see him," I protested. "Can we try?"

"It may be dangerous, but if the Eternal Being has brought you this far, perhaps He will show us a way. It is too late for us to leave today. We will leave in the morning, but we must watch the weather closely. We have a 'signal one' storm alert."

The Philippines weather bureau, I'd been told, use a three-stage warning system to denote the onset of a typhoon, or *bagyo* as they call it. Signal one indicated that a typhoon might strike within seventy-two hours. While I was concerned about the possibility of a storm, I could not—would not—let it interfere with my desire to find Lou. I had to get the answers I was seeking.

By the time we arrived at Mario's, the rain had intensified, and our clothes were soaked as we raced into his house. Mario offered me a towel, and we stood in his tiny kitchen and dried ourselves. I used the opportunity to quiz him about Lou.

"How did you come to know him?" I asked.

Mario removed his shirt and hung it on a chair to dry. I followed, pulling up another chair and sitting down.

"I will make some tea," he said.

As the water heated, he told me about the healer. "My father," he said, "also practiced the healing ways and introduced me to Eleuterio when I was a small boy. He had taught my father long before I was born."

105

"How old is he?" I asked. "When I was here before, I could hardly keep up, yet he appears to be in his sixties."

"I do not know his age. He is very old, but I have never asked. I recall him from my youth and he appears today much the same as then. We place little significance upon a person's age, knowing that we are as old or as young as we accept ourselves to be."

"That's impossible! If you knew him as a boy, he could be in his eighties. I may not be in the best shape, but I can't believe I have difficulty keeping up with a man almost twice my age. What's his secret?"

"There is no secret, only the knowledge that you are what you envision. If you see yourself as old, crippled, and unable to function, you will be. However, if you hold a positive and healthy vision of yourself, you will experience good health. You may remain active for many years beyond the number accepted as customary. We consider your willingness to accept aging, disease, and misfortune to be unusual traits that are learned in error, not through an awareness of truth."

"The problem is," I responded. "It's never black and white. Oh, it's great to discuss the possibility of a life without aging or disease, but how can you show me what I must do in order to achieve such a state of awareness? I've heard all this before. All the self-help books written during the past fifty-years have focused upon the same concepts, but none of them, not one, has offered any concrete method by which the average person could actually reach such a state."

I leaned back in my chair and began to rock back and forth. All the frustrations and hopelessness of a lifetime began to surface.

"It drives me crazy," I said, "that so-called enlightened people think they can show me how to be what I envision or that I can be anything other than what I am. I don't mean to offend you, but I guess I'm just sick of all the positive thinking propaganda. I haven't seen anyone dramatically alter their life through such thinking or visualization.

"Sure I've seen some impressive healings, things I can't explain, but there's no consistency. Nothing I've seen has shown me how to control my body or convinced me that such control is possible."

"Dan, my friend, your beliefs do not allow you to see life as it is. If you haven't seen it, for you it doesn't exist. I understand your frustration, but I can assure you that there is another world out there, another reality that you can both contact and utilize in your search for meaning. I think, after all, that your whole problem revolves around your search. When you are able to see that there is no meaning outside of yourself for you to discover, then you can begin to live the life you seek."

Mario grabbed my chair and stopped the rocking. He paused and looked toward the window, rattling as the rain beat against it.

"There is no meaning I can give to your life," he said. "I can only present you with certain experiences. It is for you to decide what those experiences mean. If you perceive your life as insignificant, it is because you have failed to see the significance of the myriad and wondrous events in the world around you."

"Look, Mario. I'm impressed by your healing methods and think Mike can help a lot of people by merging your techniques with those of modern medicine. But I don't believe the method of treatment makes a difference in the lives of those being treated, other than whether or not their disease is cured. Their healing may be dependent upon their expectations, but it makes no difference in their life. I'm sorry. I don't understand your point."

Mario stared into my eyes without speaking. He leaned forward and tapped on my forehead. "The answers are simple," he said. "But they will not come from others. They are here and you must discover them yourself. Others may help you along the way, but ultimately, you are on your own. When you are ready to accept your answers, you will discover the questions you must ask. Such discovery sometimes takes many years. And most importantly of all, there are no answers for questions such as yours. Your questions demonstrate your inability to accept the answers you seek.

"You have spent half a lifetime," he said, "lost in the dream of life. What you have seen is not real. It is but a theatrical, a play. What you see here is also a part of the play, but it is very important, for it connects you with the other, the real world."

"Explain to me," I said. "What is the connection with your so-called real world? How does healing fit in, and if it's not real, what's the use?"

"We are all part of the One. Everything is connected. It is our divine nature to care for our brothers and sisters and to heal ourselves. If we recognize a part of the whole that is not expressing its virtue, it is our duty to do what we can to bring that part into alignment. The healing, of itself, is unimportant. The significance lies in our constant striving to recognize our perfect nature. The perfection is always there. What is sometimes missing is our awareness of the perfection in all things.

"There is uncertainty in your eyes," he said. "I fear I am not a good teacher. If you reach Eleuterio, perhaps he will help you. Now it is late; we should sleep."

Mario insisted that I sleep on his bed, and he took a small couch in the living area. His huge feet extended well beyond the end, and though I protested, he would not allow me to change with him.

"You are my guest," he said. "You must have the best my humble home can offer."

I undressed and lay across the bed. Though I was exhausted, I had difficulty going to sleep. I kept thinking about what Mario had said. Perhaps he was right. I didn't feel any closer to finding what I'd been seeking than when we had first begun our discussion, and I was unable to make sense of any of it. Maybe it didn't matter anyway.

I had an uneasy sleep, waking many times and wondering why I'd returned. If I needed to discover the answers on my own, how could Lou help me?

Morning came with dark gray clouds hanging low over the city, but it wasn't raining. Mario prepared us a breakfast of bread and cheese and we were soon on our way.

We rode for miles in silence. Mario seemed to acknowledge my need to reflect. It seemed strange the way I'd been drawn to the Philippines. I wondered what I could learn in such a primitive land.

As the city disappeared behind us, a steady rain began to beat against the windshield. The wind had picked up, rocking the car and lashing at the trees along the roadside. The rain dampened my spirits, and the gray sky reflected the confusion and frustration permeating my being.

"We must take a different route," Mario said. He spun the car onto a narrow dirt road. "We will go around the mountain. The road of our last trip is too dangerous and will not be repaired until the end of the rainy season."

I was glad Mario was driving for the sky had grown black and I could hardly see the road ahead. I peered through the window. The road we had taken was narrow, little wider than the car. In places it was nearly blocked by large bushes leaning into our path.

By late afternoon I was wondering if I would be able to find Lou. What if he was off on one of his trips? Worse, what if he couldn't help with

109

any of my questions? However, something inside forced me to go on, the same urging that had driven me to return to the Philippines. It was as if some part of me knew I would find relief, if not answers. I hoped so.

Suddenly, Mario slammed on the brakes and I was thrown against the dash. "We cannot continue," he said. "The rain is too heavy and there is danger of mudslides. We must go back."

"We can't," I protested. "We're almost there. I have to see Lou."

"I am sorry, my friend, but I cannot risk our lives for this. You do not understand the danger."

"I'm willing to take that risk," I said. "I may be risking my life if I don't continue."

Without warning, the car jerked sideways, and I could feel the road moving beneath us. I was thrown against the door.

"Mudslide!" Mario yelled.

I reached out to brace myself. Before my hand could make contact, the car began a sickening roll, tumbling towards the river below. Panic gripped me and thoughts of death raced through my mind.

The car must have rolled over five or six times when my door flew open and I was thrown into a sea of mud. For a moment, there was intense pain in my left foot, then I was engulfed in blackness. Though I was unable to see, I felt my body sliding down the embankment.

My mind returned to a time, years earlier, when I'd almost drowned. I'd gone swimming with some of my teenage friends and been caught in a severe undertow. The same strange feeling of quiet wrapped me in its wet, sticky cocoon, and I lost consciousness.

I awoke to see a bright light before me, brighter than any light I'd ever seen. I was free, alive, I thought. I felt great. I couldn't believe I had no injuries. I looked around to see where I was, but could see nothing except light.   The realization came to me that I must be dead.   What I was experiencing could not be life.

There was no pain, no physical sensations at all, not as I normally experienced.   I was in a dimension that defied my concept of reality. Nothing seemed real, yet on some level, everything was more real, more substantial, than anything I accepted as life. I wasn't sure where I was, but I felt unusually secure.

The light grew brighter and I moved toward it. So this was death. At least it was painless.

A face appeared out of the light and I recognized it immediately as Lou. "You're not dead," I said. "You can't be here."

The face smiled and spoke, "No, I am not dead and neither are you."

The image disappeared, everything went black, and I began to hear a dull roar, like the sound of an airplane passing overhead. I focused upon the sound and tried to identify it, to connect with it, and as I tried, I felt sensations in my body.   There was a strange coldness in my left arm, then my leg. Soon, the sound and the accompanying cold surrounded my body.

I was in the river! I was very much alive and being dragged by the current. I struggled to keep my head above the surface. I was shoved into the side of a huge boulder and remained there, held fast by the current, while the icy water rushed past, tearing at my body.

My hands clawed at the sides of the rock, as I tried to pull free. Slowly, painfully, I inched forward until I dragged myself over the boulder and onto the rocks lining the shore.

I was safe—exhausted, in pain, and bleeding—but safe. The rain beating against my back felt wonderful. I was grateful to be alive. I savored every drop that pounded me and reaffirmed my existence.

My attention shifted to my foot. It ached. I remembered the pain I'd felt when I was thrown from the car. The car! My God! Where was the car? Where was Mario?

I rose up and looked around. I could see across the river where my ordeal had begun. In the twilight I could just make out the remains of the road, high above me, with a fifty-foot long section gone, an open gash in the side of the mountain. I scanned the riverbank, the river, but there was no sign of Mario or his car. I was sure he was either buried under the mountains of mud or had been swept away by the current. Either option meant that he was dead.

I felt an overwhelming sadness, aware that I was the reason for his death. My insane mission, my craving for knowledge, had cost the life of a friend, a friend who deserved life much more than I did. I cursed my foolish inquisitiveness for causing me to think I would ever find the answers I sought. What difference did it make if I understood or not? What good would my knowing bring to the world?

I collapsed into the mud, head in my hands, and cried. I had yet another example of my worthless existence. I was a misfit, creating chaos and destruction at every turn.

Hours seemed to have passed when I felt a hand on my shoulder, and I jerked around as someone called my name. "Mario," I said. "I thought you were dead."

A dark figure stood before me, but it was not Mario. It was Lou. Somehow, through the rain, the flooding, the mudslide, Lou had found me. He reached down and lifted me from the mud.

I forgot the accident, the loss of my friend, and the reasons for my return to find Lou. I felt a quiet peace, at one with something much larger than my trivial experiences.

But as suddenly as the feeling of well-being appeared, it vanished as Lou released me from his grasp. All my fears, my insecurities, all my questions reappeared, and I yelled out in pain as I remembered my foot.

I stared into his eyes. His piercing gaze burned into my soul. I felt naked, unable to conceal my thoughts.

Lou broke the silence. "Well, my friend, you return to our country. Did you not find my answers satisfactory?"

"Mario . . . Mario is dead. There was a mudslide."

"No," Lou said. "He is not dead. He is with friends down the river. He did say he had a very interesting ride."

"W . . . What? How?" I asked.

"It seems that his car was washed downstream, and Mario was able to climb out before it disappeared into the river. He is fine, but we may not see him for a time."

"You saw him?" I asked.

"No, not as you understand."

"I don't understand at all," I said. "If you didn't see him, how could he tell you these things?"

"Don't be so inquisitive, my friend. There are things and experiences your rational mind will not allow you to accept. You must first cleanse your thinking of the ideas you hold about the world you believe you experience. You have much to forget."

He motioned for me to follow. "Come. We should find you some dry clothes. You are quite a mess."

I tried to walk, but the pain in my foot was too severe. I stumbled and grabbed a tree for support.

Lou put his arm around my shoulder and pulled me along the riverbank. "I will look at your foot when we reach my home," he said.

After walking about a hundred yards, we turned and climbed a steep and barely visible trail that led to the ridge above.

Though I was in pain, I felt safe. However, I would soon discover the limits of my fear where I would become more insecure, more vulnerable than ever. I had no idea of the dangers I would encounter.

CHAPTER 9

DEATH OF SELF

Lou helped me as I struggled along the rugged trail to his house. Each step was agony. Though I had to stop and rest several times, Lou seemed invigorated, once more amazing me with his stamina. For him the hike seemed easy, and he practically carried me along. Fortunately for my foot, the trip was relatively short, as Mario had driven us much closer than on my first visit, and we walked for no more than an hour.

We arrived at the house as the forest became enshrouded in darkness. I couldn't have walked much more and was thankful we didn't have to hike the trail after dark.

The place was much as I remembered, small, secluded, and terribly neglected. However, there was one noticeable difference. Most of the roof was gone and had been replaced with a bright blue canvas.

When I asked him about the damage, Lou laughed and said, "Yes, Spirit has given me a convertible. When the weather is good, I can sleep with the stars and share my home with the birds and other creatures. Is it not wonderful?"

Wonderful would not have been my adjective of choice, but then, I didn't share Lou's feelings or understanding in other areas either. As I looked around the room—or what remained of it—I could see that most of Lou's belongings had been moved into the corner sheltered by the remaining roof. In the opposite corner, birds nested on a shelf that had once extended over Lou's cot. One more storm, I thought, and the place would return to nature.

"Yeah, it's great," I said.

That was the first time we had talked since leaving the river. When I was not focused upon my pain, I'd tried to break down my questions and doubts into a rational format I could use to describe my dilemma.

I had not yet decided how to phrase my questions when Lou asked, "Why did you return? What do you expect to discover in these mountains?"

"Answers," I said. "I want answers to questions that have bothered me since my first experience with miracle healings in Arizona. I want to know why it's so difficult for me to have the things, spiritual things, I see in others. I've tried, yet see others like you and Mario, who seem to easily experience a world to which I've been excluded. I want to understand what's going on and why—why your healings aren't more common in the civil . . . uh, modern world."

I bent down to remove my hiking boots. My foot was swollen, making it both difficult and painful to get the boot off. I was sure something was broken.

"I understand," he said. "You think your world is more civilized, more intellectual than the world of these uneducated and backward people who, in their ignorance, are forced to rely upon myth and superstition for healing purposes. You see the success of our methods, and yet, you continue to feel your way is superior because it comes from science. Yet, much of science is based in theory. Is it not?"

He instructed me to sit on the floor in front of him. As I leaned against the wall, he carefully examined my foot. I winced with each movement and tried to block out the pain radiating up my leg.

"I believe your methods work," I said. "I've seen it."

"It appears that you will get an even closer look at our healing methods, my friend." He stood and looked down at me. "You have broken your foot."

"What can I do?" I asked. "I need to get back home and finish the book. Even if it's possible, I don't think I have the faith necessary to accept a miracle."

"No, you do not. You lack the understanding that brings acceptance. Your use of the word 'miracle' indicates your failure to accept what you have seen as natural. You see our healings as aberrations, beyond the realm of nature, yet the opposite is true. Your inability to see the true meaning is the aberration. You wish to examine the process and discover a scientific explanation, but I tell you, science cannot explain the workings of Spirit."

Lou stepped to his cupboard, retrieved a small metal container, and sat on the floor in front of me. He supported my foot with one hand and began applying a thick brown salve with the other. My skin tingled as he briskly massaged my foot and ankle. Within seconds the pain lessened, and he began slow stroking motions with his fingers lightly touching my skin, beginning at my knee and moving down across my foot. As he worked he continued to explain.

"Your technological age has produced great advancements," he said. "But they have come at a terrible cost. You have made science your god and look to science with the expectation that it will supply your needs and bring answers. The current practice of medicine is typical of man's misdirection. Advancements in medicine have led man far from true healing into a complete dependence upon surgery and the use of synthetic drugs."

After instructing me to close my eyes, Lou continued working with my foot for about ten minutes. When he had finished, he stood and walked over to one of the boxes stacked in the corner. After rummaging through the box, he produced a shirt and a pair of pants. "Put these on," he said.

As I struggled to my feet, I noticed that the pain had lessened considerably. The throbbing had stopped and I was able to stand without help from Lou.

"It is interesting to note," he said, returning to our conversation, "the slight renewal of interest in the old ways. However, I fear it may be too late to save the world from the destruction that was begun as we lost touch with our true nature and with nature, itself. The awakening to the spiritual side of man is good, but only time will tell whether the purpose of man's rediscovered spirituality is to extend his life on earth or to prepare him for life in the next."

He walked over and faced me, placing both his hands on my shoulders. Peace and contentment radiated from him. I looked around the room. It's all relative, I thought. I complain about living on Conquest, how things get wet when it rains, and how I lack sufficient space. Yet, here was Lou, living under conditions that most would consider deplorable, and finding happiness in each circumstance.

"I do not know the purpose of man's awakening spirituality," he said. "And the answer is unimportant. Spirit knows the best course, and whatever occurs will help advance man toward his ultimate goal of reunion with his true self."

"What you are saying," I interrupted, "is fine for us to consider and for monks to meditate upon. Mario told me the same thing, but it's confusing. I don't believe I can ever fully understand the nature of man and his relationship with the Divine. My spirit is wounded more than my foot, and regardless of how I medicate it, I can't seem to effect a healing. I can't imagine how you can maintain a state of bliss when your world seems to be in such a state of collapse."

"Dan, you are in conflict with your developing spirituality and are filled with self-pity. You want me to feel sorry for your plight. I do not. Though you may not find the answers you seek, you will find answers; but your search will never end. It is within your search that you will find the meaning you seek. There is not one ultimate answer to be discovered, but a process of continual growth and evolution."

As I pulled on the dry trousers, Lou motioned for me to sit in one of his two chairs. I sat down, wiping the mud from my face and arms. I thought about what he had said. Maybe I would find meaning in my life. I needed some.

Somewhere, deep inside my mind I felt that something positive was happening, but I was reluctant to acknowledge the feeling, afraid it might go away. I thought about Ted and wished he could see me. His persistence had possibly changed the direction of my life. I owed him a sincere and significant debt of gratitude. I smiled and turned toward Lou as he began to speak.

"Your ego causes you to feel that your conscious self can find the way to enlightenment, that if you work hard enough or find the right teacher your mind will understand. You must recognize your true self and stop attempting to control the direction of your life. Instead, allow your life to unfold in harmony with your growing awareness. Once you acknowledge self and know that you are one with all things, there will be no need for ego, no need to raise yourself above others. You will discover that there are no others, separate from you, to rise above.

"Your mind paints a picture of a world of opposites—good and evil, right and wrong, sadness and happiness, love and hate. However, all are part of the same. Everything is Spirit. Once you understand that it is only your perceptions which cause you to divide things into opposites, you will be released from fear, from your pursuit of happiness, and from your futile search for love."

He paused for a moment, allowing me to absorb what he had said. "You must rest," he said. "Your foot needs some time to heal and you must prepare for the work to come."

Pointing to his cot, he said, "Sleep. There will be more time for questions tomorrow."

I hopped over to his cot and collapsed in exhaustion. The events of the day had taken their toll and both my body and mind needed a reprieve. I was asleep within minutes.

During the night I dreamed I heard the call of the strange bird that had circled Conquest. I felt as if I were its prey. I saw it flying toward me, flapping its giant wings and grabbing me with claws that tore my flesh. The dream faded as the creature carried me toward a rendezvous with death.

The next morning I awoke to feel water dripping onto my face. It was raining heavily and the roof and canvas leaked in several places. I looked around the room, amazed by the manner in which Lou accepted his plight. I wondered if I would ever attain such serenity.

My strange sleep had left me feeling wonderfully refreshed, and I leaped out of bed, having forgotten my broken foot. As I stood, remembering the discomfort of the night before, I grimaced and leaned against the wall in anticipation of the pain I was sure would come. There was no pain! My foot felt great, as if nothing had happened. Maybe it hadn't been as serious as I'd thought.

Above the sound of the wind and rain I heard Lou. He was singing. I walked to the door and found him seated at the edge of the porch. He looked up and smiled. "How is your foot?" he asked.

I was sure he knew the answer, but I responded. "It's great, no pain at all."

"Good," he said.

I didn't know how much Lou had helped my foot. Perhaps it had only been a sprain. For some reason, although I'd already seen some remarkable healings, I couldn't accept one for myself. I didn't question Lou about what he had done. Instead, I changed the subject.

"Last night," I said. "You were talking about everything being the same. You said that good and evil, love and hate are all parts of Spirit, that there's no difference. How do you explain that? What about all the bad things I've experienced? They sure make me feel different, feel worse than the good things."

"You must give up your beliefs in a structured, material world," he said. "That is the great sacrifice in the realization of Oneness. The evils you despise, which bring you fear and which cause you great sadness, are nothing. You must know, however, that the happiness and tranquility you seek is also nothing, no more than the opposites they reflect. All is Spirit. You create the separation that causes your confusion. There is nothing to fear. There is nothing to gain. Recognize everything as Spirit and you will be free."

"Look," I said. "I came here to understand the process and the meaning of healing, of life. What can I do to understand?"

"Americans," he sighed. "Do you expect instant enlightenment? You speed through life, searching for quick answers and meaning. Life is not a maze to be conquered and there is no shortcut, no easy remedy to your struggle. Be cautious, my friend. Shortcuts often lead to a dead end.

"Time, as you know it, does not exist. Yet, you place time limits upon everything and find disappointment and despair when your quick answers do not come. Release the need to know and knowledge will come. Release the attachment to outcomes and happiness will come. Stop seeking and you will find the enlightenment you desire. Until you do so, you will remain in your pitiful state."

Lou looked toward the forest. The noise of the wind and rain made it difficult to hear him. I stepped closer.

"There are no answers that will lead you to enlightenment," he said. "Perhaps I may direct you, may remove some of the obstacles that block your path, but I cannot travel it with you. I can show you my path, but it will not lead you to your goal. Listen to your inner voice."

He paused as if searching for the right words. "Dan, Spirit has brought us together for a purpose, a purpose you and I may not fully understand. Remain open, receptive to everything you see and feel and you will achieve a state of understanding that will rid you of your need for answers. You will no longer be distracted by the illusion you call life.

"We must now cleanse your mind in preparation for the wisdom you seek. As your body is filled with toxins from your environment and poor diet, your mind is congested with the debris of an unenlightened life."

Lou pointed to a rocky ledge about a quarter of a mile away. "Go and sit," he said. "Stay until you can let go. You must release your attachment to illusion."

"Am I to meditate?" I asked.

"Go and sit. What you seek will find you. Enlightenment does not come through effort, but from the release of effort. Go."

"What about the storm?" I asked. "Can I find some shelter? There's a typhoon coming."

"Go, now."

I didn't understand what Lou wanted me to do. What purpose would sitting on a rock in a driving rainstorm accomplish? I turned and walked toward the outcropping he'd pointed out.

Climbing to the top was not as easy as it had appeared from the safety of Lou's porch. The rocks were slippery and few places offered sound footing.

When I reached the top, I slid over to the ledge as Lou had instructed. The height was unnerving. However, if it had not been for the clouds and rain, the place would have offered a spectacular view of the mountains and valley before me. In better weather it would have been a great place to reflect.

I located a section of the rock where I could sit and rest my back against the side of large boulder. Leaning against the rock provided stability and helped me feel secure. As I stretched my legs, I wondered what I would learn from Lou's bizarre teaching methods.

My shirt and trousers were drenched, and I wondered why Lou had bothered giving me a change of clothes. The rain, driven by gale force winds, quickly penetrated to my skin and I shivered uncontrollably.

What was I doing? I felt like an idiot for following Lou's orders so willingly. There had to be an easier way. But I wanted to cooperate. I needed to trust him. There was no other option. I hoped his bizarre methods would be of some value.

I remembered something he had said: "Enlightenment does not come through effort, but from the release of effort." I waited. Nothing happened. I didn't feel enlightened. I was wet and miserable.

Wiping the rain from my forehead, I looked toward the horizon. Thoughts appeared, distracting me from my purpose, and I tried to ignore them. Each time I became aware I was focused upon a specific thought, I attempted to clear my mind.

I drifted through a maze of confused ideas and visions, some of which were familiar. Many were not. I viewed the scenes before me as an observer, detached from my visions, yet connected in a way I cannot describe. I felt alone, abandoned, and helpless.

Peering down at the rocks, I watched as water collected into small puddles that streamed over the side. From the corner of my eye I detected movement and turned as a huge beetle crawled out of its shelter and crept toward me, oblivious to the rain. The thing was at least three inches long with two giant claws protruding from the sides of its head. It climbed across my shoe and up my trousers, stopping at my waist. I felt a primitive connection with my grotesque companion and was drawn into its gaze. On some level, I knew it felt connected to me.

I looked into its tiny black eyes for what could have been hours, hypnotized by their stillness. Unaware of the rain, unaware of my position on the rock, I was lost in an absence of thought.

At some point, I felt the sensation of rising, pulling away from my body. I was conscious, and yet, when I looked around, I could see my body sitting in the rain! My consciousness and my vision were detached from my body. But how could I observe myself?

My sudden separation from my body didn't startle me, but felt natural as I floated over the cliff and trees below. The sensations I experienced were dramatically different from those I had in the confines of my physical body, and I savored each moment of my wondrous flight.

I sailed over the trees in the direction of Lou's cabin and sensed myself gradually lowering towards earth. As I drew near I saw him seated at his table, looking towards the door. When I was within earshot, he spoke.

"Have you found answers?" he asked.

I couldn't understand why he wasn't shocked by my sudden appearance and wondered if the experience might be some sort of altered state. Perhaps he had hypnotized me. Nevertheless, I answered. "I don't know what questions to ask," I said.

"Good," he said. "You are seeing the illusion."

He reached out and grabbed my arm and the room went black. I had the sensation of moving at great speed, although I could see nothing. The feeling reminded me of how I'd felt during the mudslide. I panicked.

Although I couldn't see him, I heard Lou's voice once more. "I will show you the debris that has clouded your mind," he said.

My sight returned, and a house appeared before me, my house. But it wasn't from the present. What I saw was the home I'd lived in as a boy, and though I don't recall how I did it, I was soon standing in the kitchen, which appeared as it had forty years before. I saw my mother and was drawn to her. Standing there, I felt love— unconditional love—radiating all around. I'd never before acknowledged, never given love that was so all-encompassing. In that moment I could see how my ego and selfishness had directed my life.

The love I'd expressed had been conditional, given only when something was offered in return. Such love was artificial, unable to withstand the rigorous trials of human existence. I saw that there were not different degrees of love; there was only one love, which seemed to bind together everything in the universe.

Though I heard no voice, something spoke inside me and I knew the message was true. "Love is the key. All else is formed in love. Without it, there is no earth, no life, no man."

I was desperate to tell my mother I loved her, that I understood how she had loved me, but I could not. It was as if I were a prisoner in a cell created by my own ignorance. I tried to speak, to cry out her name, but my voice was locked within my throat.

I'd been unaware of Lou's presence and was startled by his voice. "There is more for you to see," he said. He pointed to the door into the study.

Inside, my father was seated at his massive mahogany desk, addressing a young boy. He spoke in a loud voice, and the boy shuffled his feet, staring at the floor.

"Young man," he said. "You are preparing to go away to boarding school where you will see new things and have new experiences. Remember that you, and only you, can control your life. Never let yourself fall victim to the deceptions of this world. Never let others see your weakness, your fear; and you will maintain an advantage that will allow you to rise above your fellow man.

"When you are hurt, do not cry. When you are afraid, show your strength. While others are struggling with their weakness, you will stand alone, above the mediocrity of this world. You are Daniel Murphy. You have a destiny no man can keep you from attaining."

He was talking to me! I was the young boy, trembling before his father. Observing that scene I recalled how my father had always pressured me to excel, to be the best, and how I'd never equaled his expectations.

I recalled his reaction to my test scores. Even those times I did well, he seemed dissatisfied. My grades were never good enough. I remembered his denunciation when I wasn't named valedictorian of my class. I'd been pleased that my grades were better than one hundred-fifty other students, but he had chided me saying: "If you are satisfied with second best, you will never succeed in life; and I certainly don't intend to support someone who doesn't do their best. No one remembers the one who places second. Only the best are respected and remembered."

That was the first time I'd reconsidered my father's plans of following him into the medical profession. I resented his domineering attitude and rebelled at the control he maintained upon my life, yet his presence had haunted me into adulthood.

Lou's voice startled me, erasing the vision from my mind. "It is time to go," he said. "You have other things to see."

As quickly as he had spoken, he was gone, and I felt myself moving again. I sensed I was returning to the rocky ledge where my strange vision had begun. Though I couldn't see, I felt myself settling back onto the stone. It seemed as if many hours had passed.

My body was rigid and I became aware that my eyes were tightly closed. I opened them and peered into the rain. Raising my hand to protect my eyes, I wiped the water from my face, and strained to see something that would anchor my thoughts. I thought about the vision I'd had.

My life had been a series of attempts to excel, a constant struggle to meet my father's expectations. Yet in each new venture I'd sown the seeds of failure and destruction.

Examining my past allowed me to see how my direction had been determined in an almost masochistic fashion. I'd become lost in my attempts to achieve goals that were always beyond my grasp.

I wondered if I could change. What could I do that would allow me to see, to experience the fullness of a life without pain? What was missing? What would help me understand so that I might find peace?

The rain had become a solid wall of water that beat against my body and tore at my clothes. When I could endure the torment no longer, I stood and looked for shelter under one of the large boulders protruding from the side of the mountain. My beetle companion had disappeared, returned to the safety of its nest. I searched for some way to lower myself from the ledge.

As I leaned out, a powerful gust blew against my chest, and I fell to my knees, sliding to the edge of the precipice. The wind was a deafening roar that seemed conscious and sinister in its attempt to destroy me. I tried to check my slide, but each movement caused me to lose more of my grasp.

I called for Lou, but my cries were swallowed in the fury of the wind and rain and seemed to vanish upon leaving my throat. I thought of the life I'd wasted, having only begun to understand how to live. I would never benefit from the knowledge I'd so recently gained.

I thought of Mike and my work on the book, another task I'd failed to complete. I'd never contributed to life. I was a misfit, a taker, lost in a world in which I'd been unable to adapt.

Clinging to the rock seemed meaningless. What purpose could saving my life accomplish, and who would I save it for? I had lived my life as if something could be gained through focused attention upon self, an insult to everyone and everything in my experience. I no longer cared about myself, no longer wanted to live.

I recalled a Bible verse I'd learned as a child, a verse from *Mark*, "For whosoever shall lose his life shall save it." Yes, lose my life. I was ready to lose my life. And somewhere, above the sound of the wind and rain, I heard Lou, "Let go," he said. "Release your hold on illusion. Let go."

My strength was gone. My will to live, which for months had grown weaker, was gone, and I released my hold on the rocks. As I slipped over the edge, I felt myself falling, spinning, but I had no fear. I was more calm than ever before. For the first time in my life I knew peace.

I lost all sense of time and could have fallen for hours, immersed in feelings I'd never before experienced. I didn't care where I was or who I had been and no longer felt contempt toward my previous life. For a brief moment, I was saddened that I'd learned too late how to release from my attachment to the physical, how to recognize the only things of importance, and how to experience love.

I didn't think about death, certain death, my death, that would come the instant I reached the rocks below. Once again I heard Lou's voice, "See the illusion. Nothing is as you envision it to be. Open your eyes."

I don't know if it was Lou's direction or the sudden realization that the valley floor was coming up awfully fast, but something caused me to open my eyes. For an instant the earth appeared before me, and I caught a brief glimpse of the trees and boulders at the bottom of the ravine. My body became rigid, anticipating collision with the ground.

The impact I felt, however, was more like diving into a pool of warm water as my body plunged beneath the earth's crust. I'm not certain whether my eyes were opened or closed, but I had the sensation of being engulfed in darkness as I continued to sink deeper underground, terrified and unable to breath. Every muscle was drawn tight, paralyzed by fear and the suffocating pressure I felt.

Just as I thought I would lose consciousness, I catapulted to the surface, choking and gasping for air. My body shook violently and I had the sensation of pressure on my shoulder. Where was I? Why was I conscious?

I opened my eyes, afraid of what I might see. In my dazed condition I could just make out the figure standing over me, shaking me and calling my name. It was Lou.

"Dan," he said. "You are dreaming."

"Huh? What's going on?" I asked. I was unable to focus my vision or my thoughts.

"It appears you were dreaming."

"B . . . but I fell . . . the cliff. I don't understand."

"You fell?" he asked. "How did you get here?"

I looked around. I'd returned to the safety of Lou's house and was lying on his cot.

"I don't know how I got here," I said. "I fell off the cliff, into the earth, but I wasn't dreaming. And my clothes, look at them. They're covered with mud."

Lou frowned. "Yes, that is how you judge reality. If it feels real, then it must be, like the magazine you said I left on your boat. You said it was real, but you could not produce it when I asked to see it. Have you not changed your vision?"

"Look," I said. "I don't know how you did it—the boat or the fall—but I know you're involved. You're hypnotizing me or something."

"Now you say I have hypnotized you. I think you have a vivid imagination, my friend. Do you think it is possible that you could have done it yourself? You give me too much credit."

"Don't make jokes about this," I said. "I think I'm losing my mind."

"I cannot help but laugh at your situation," he responded. "You take everything so seriously."

"Okay, I don't understand. Will you explain it for me?" I pleaded.

"Yes," he responded. I could detect true kindness in his voice. "I will explain as I understand, but I may not provide the answers you seek."

"Tell me what happened. Am I dead or alive?"

"Oh, I think you are very much alive," he answered. "And very wet."

Lou pulled a blanket from the end of his cot and wrapped it around my trembling body. But the blanket could not stop the shivering that came more from anxiety than cold.

"What you experienced," Lou began, "was necessary because you have such a powerful attachment to your illusion of life. You would not have understood if I had told you about it. You are very stubborn in your beliefs. It will take strong measures to bring you to an understanding of what your life is about."

"What made me feel that I fell off the cliff if I did not?" I asked. "Was I hypnotized?"

"I did not say that you did not fall," he said. "But you were not hypnotized, not in the way you ask. Your experience of a fall assisted you in your search for truth."

"Did I fall or not?" I asked. "What happened?"

"You attempt to fit everything into your old and very limited vision. Let go of your beliefs. You do not understand reality, for there is no one single reality. There are many. Forget the old and open your mind to the boundless possibilities that exist for you. And yes, a part of you did fall, and that part is now dead.

"There are three very important things you must know, three things which are keys to further knowledge," he continued. "First, you must know that all is illusion. The very thing you came here to learn, healing, is illusion, and so is disease. Nothing is real unless you accept it as so. Your illusion tells you that we live and die, but it is only the illusion that lives and dies.

"The storm outside, your fall, the failure of you marriage, your inability to find success, are all illusion. However, it is not illusion as you understand it. Illusion means that one holds no more power than the other. Good is no better than evil. Love, as you understand it, no better than hate. Light, no better than darkness. All are the same and are parts of our creation of life."

"Tell me about my fall. How did I create that?"

"The fall helped prepare you for what I am telling you now and for what is to come. If we had talked one year ago, would you have believed me? Could you accept my words?"

"I have to know," I pressed harder. "Did I fall or not? And if I didn't, where did the experience come from?"

Lou paced back and forth as he responded. "The answer is part of the illusion. You experienced falling, as you perceive breath and life. Your mind tells you that you fell, but the mind and the body are only vibrations. What you experienced was a change in the vibration, a change that you find very different and difficult to comprehend, and you want me to confirm that your body—which you believe to be solid—fell off the cliff. You think that if you observe something in the physical, then it is real, but I will tell you that there is no difference between what you would call the physical and the dream you had of falling. All is illusion."

"But if everything is illusion," I argued, "then nothing matters, and it makes no difference what I do or say. I could kill someone and it wouldn't matter. Right?"

"You have confused your concept of illusion with true illusion. The answer is that it does not make a difference. You think it would; therefore, it would—for you. Your vision of life is that your so-called misdeeds make you imperfect or evil and keep you from attaining your destiny of perfection, but the opposite is true. Each of your deeds helps to fulfill your destiny. Each action brings you closer to your realization of perfection.

"All is important, because it is important to you, but makes no difference to the ultimate plan for all things. You decide what is important. You make your choices. Sometimes your choice may be not to choose."

Lou placed his hands on my temples. A powerful surge of electricity passed through me. "You are holding on to your old concepts of reality and illusion. Create your reality, NOW!"

As he spoke, a beautiful young woman appeared in front of me. She seemed as real as either Lou or I, and her deep brown eyes gazed into mine. A chill ran through me, and I could feel the tingling sensation of hairs standing on end.

The woman looked at me with a smile that conveyed caring, love, and understanding. Although her lips never moved, I heard her speak. "You are kind and can do much to return love and understanding into a world that has lost its vision. I am honored to meet you. Perhaps we may meet again when you have awakened from your dream."

Lou removed his hands from my head and the girl vanished. I looked around the room to see where she had gone.

"That's what I mean," I said. "How did you do that?"

"That is precisely what I mean," he responded. "The experience was yours. You created it. I merely helped to remove the obstructions that keep you from realizing the fullness of life. Your experiences are limited by past conditioning. You have been told that what you just saw is impossible, and until now, you accepted that judgment. Now, you are free to participate in a life that is filled with magic and wonder. If you can release yourself from your old beliefs, you will observe many such wonders."

"But I can't just say that the things I've learned, that I've experienced, don't exist. How can I change my perception?" I asked.

"You have already begun to change." he said. "You are seeing and experiencing a new reality, and you are searching to understand what you have seen and what you now know to be possible. Your search began many years ago, and you have built upon the results of that search. It is true that, 'As you seek, so you will find.' True initiates are no different from you. They have learned to be sensitive to their experiences, and," He paused and took a small stone from his pocket, holding it before me. "They look for meaning in all things."

He placed the stone in my palm and closed my fingers around it. "Dan, you think you are unworthy of the understanding I describe, but, like the stone, I know you to be a perfect representation of Spirit. You only need

134

to recognize your perfection. The way for you, for all, is to quiet the mind and look within. Your constant chattering blocks out the truth you seek. Be still. Listen. Then you will know.

"I cannot tell you that if you will meditate in a special way or that if you will perform certain rituals, you will receive enlightenment, for I cannot describe what I know, and cannot touch the part of you that must know. However, I can direct you to a path that leads to understanding, and I can help you to open your mind to the possibilities that exist. If you will listen with your heart, seeking your highest good, you will know. No one can keep you from the ecstasy of spiritual awakening."

"You mentioned a connection with all things," I said. "I can't comprehend that. I understand how things are based in energy, but how does that connect me with a stone or a bird? What difference does it make if there is a connection?"

"Yes, Oneness with all things is the second key to enlightenment. Once you can see your connection with all things, it will be easy for you to understand that your only limitations are self-imposed. If your and this stone are one, you can experience the tranquility of a stone. If you are one with a bird, you will know the majesty of flight and can soar above the limitations of earth with a new perspective. Yes, all things are connected. All things are a part of the One, which is Spirit. When you recognize your Oneness, all things become possible."

He took a deep breath and lowered his voice. "To fully recognize Oneness is to fulfill your destiny—to reach the highest state of earth life.

"Finally," he said. "You must learn the meaning of love. When you understand illusion, when you realize your connection with all things, then, and only then. will your life be an expression of love."

CHAPTER 10

THE MIRACLE
OF ONENESS

It didn't take long to discover how love touches everything in life. For those who properly understood and expressed love, everything would to fall into place.

"Love," Lou said, "has confused man for centuries. Real love, the only true love, is born of Spirit and recognizes the perfection in all things and all people. Love rejoices when the object of that love fulfills its destiny, regardless of the path.

"When love is directed toward a person," he continued, "it cannot interfere with or be critical of their actions or beliefs. Love is acceptance. Anything else cannot be love.

"That is not to say that you should not try to help those who you believe have strayed from their path, but you can never know what is best for another. Everything has its place in the universe. Everything and everyone is trying to reach their destiny. The scorpion stings. The snake bites. That is their destiny. When we understand the meaning of love, we can accept the uniqueness of all things. None in this life are able to reach such a state of pure acceptance—of unconditional love—but we should never cease striving."

He stopped speaking and stared toward the darkness of the forest. His words had touched a part of me I didn't know existed. If only I could have known him at an earlier time. I might have avoided a lot of pain.

Without warning, I felt an intense pain in my head and the room went black. I sensed Lou was no longer with me and felt alone, helpless. Once again, time seemed to stand still.

I couldn't judge how long the condition lasted, but at some point, my vision returned. It was a gradual, almost imperceptible change, as detected a difference in the light my eyes were receiving. At first, it was only an increase in light, then I could see vague forms and shapes. Finally, I was able to make out my surroundings.

For a moment, I thought I was having another migraine—I'd not had one since Phoenix—but soon realized it was no ordinary headache. A room came into vision, but not the one I'd been sharing with Lou; this was another, vastly different, yet somehow strangely familiar. I was in the house I'd shared with Susan! I could see her at the window.

I looked around in amazement. I was sure I was dreaming, but my awareness was so strong, so vivid; it was unlike any dream I'd experienced. I was there. I could touch my surroundings, the furniture, smell the familiar aroma of the imported pipe tobacco I once smoked. Once more I'd been transported to a place and time from my past.

I tried to gain some understanding of what I was experiencing and why, and scanned the room. Susan stared out the window. I heard her soft sobbing. I'd never before identified with the pain or confusion she'd said I caused, never accepted my part in her anguish.

She turned towards me. She looked innocent, childlike, beautiful. "Why do you do this to me—to us?" she asked. "Why can't you see what you're doing to our relationship? I don't care about the money, the status. I only want us to spend time together, like we used to. What good is a house at the beach if you're gone all the time, working so we can have it? We don't need all this stuff."

The quarreling wasn't at all as I remembered. I'd placed the blame on Susan for our ever-increasing appetite for more, and had never acknowledged that I—my ego— could have been the cause for so many of our problems. But my vision provided more clarity than ever. I'd been the driving force behind our lust for things.

Susan was still looking towards me. "Why?" she asked again. Tears streamed down her cheeks. "Why?"

I wanted to respond, to let her know I realized that it was my fault, when a loud voice spoke behind me.

"You're crazy. For years we've talked about a house at the beach, and this just happens to be the buy of the century. Hell, it's a steal. With a little work, we could probably double our money in a few years. Think of it as an investment."

As I turned to see who was speaking, I felt a knot forming in my stomach, a knot of realization that I was the one causing Susan's pain. I looked into the corner to see a figure seated at a desk, my desk. It was me. I felt the contempt, the conceit, that radiated from this caricature of me. The lips were curled in an arrogant sneer. I was repulsed by the inimical glare from such a loathsome being. How could I have been so uncaring? I winced in pain, acknowledging my guilt.

"Don't be silly," this person—this me—chided. "Think of all the good times we'll have, the parties we can give. None of our friends have a vacation home."

I could sense that he didn't—I didn't—really care about spending time with Susan. I'd massaged an over-inflated ego through an accumulation of possessions. More stuff would be an indication of success. I recoiled in disgust as I looked onto the scene.

It seemed strange that I didn't recall the conversation played before me. It probably had occurred as I'd seen it, but had not been recorded in my memory. I wondered how many similar instances might have happened, other times I'd ignored Susan's pleas for reason.

I was embarrassed that Lou had seen my narcissistic display and anguished over my behavior. I didn't want to see more. Sorrow pulsated through my body and I choked back the emotions I felt.

Lou touched my shoulder. "There is no need for guilt," he said. "Guilt accomplishes nothing. What you have seen will help you understand your present plight and will help you achieve the realization of your potential. Detach from the blame and absorb the implications of what you have observed. You are learning the meaning of love, how to give and

139

receive love. Reflect, without emotional attachment, on your experiences. Love is the most important of all. Focus upon love and you will find understanding and forgiveness."

Lou's words resonated within my body producing an unusual calmness. I closed my eyes and fell into a deep sleep.

When I awoke, it appeared to be dawn. The sun streamed in through cracks in the side of Lou's house, painting narrow bands of light across the floor. I looked at my watch. It was 6:45. I lay on my side and watched the light move across the floor, beginning a slow climb up the wall on the opposite side of the room. The play of light and shadow was confusing. Something wasn't right. The sun was on the wrong side of the room. It wasn't morning. It was evening. I'd slept all day!

I jumped up, slipped on my boots, and ran to the door. Lou was nowhere in sight. I walked to the edge of the porch and called his name. There was no response and no indication of where he'd gone. I wondered what I should do.

The rain had stopped, and I walked into the edge of the forest. Huge trees cast long shadows onto the clearing. The air was alive with the calls of nocturnal animals and birds.

"Don't leave me here," I whispered. "I need your help."

Suddenly, there was movement in the bushes to my right and I spun around as a form appeared, no more than twenty feet away. "Dan," a voice called. I jumped in surprise as a young woman stepped from the shadows.

"You!" I cried, as the figure stepped closer. "I remember you. You appeared to me in a dream."

It was the beautiful young woman from my vision of the night before. But where had she come from and how did she know me?

"I am Maria," she said. "Eleuterio has asked me to bring you to him."

"Where is he?" I asked.

"He is across the mountain," she responded. Her soft voice floated from her lips.

She was small, no more than five feet, and her long hair silhouetted her tiny face. And she was beautiful, but it was more than beauty that attracted me. There was something else. Her eyes, her remarkable eyes. They had the same piercing quality I'd seen in Lou's.

"How do you know me?" I asked. "I mean, I saw you in a dream. I think it was a dream . . . and you recognized me."

"Yes, you saw me, but it was not a dream. What you think of as reality is your dream, and with Eleuterio's help, you are awakening. I am pleased to share in your journey."

"But do you know me?" I asked. "Do you know why I'm here?"

"Yes, Eleuterio has asked me to assist in you search for your path," She paused. "Perhaps you will also help me."

"I'm sorry," I said. "I'm afraid I'm too lost to help anyone. I don't know why I came here or what I'm looking for."

"We all have difficulty determining our path," she said. "And in our search we encounter others searching for theirs. By joining together we can learn from each other's experiences. We do not meet by chance. There is a purpose to be fulfilled and a destiny which must not be avoided. That is why such encounters are so important for us, for we have both the opportunity to learn and to teach."

I'd remained behind the bushes during our conversation and stepped forward; embarrassed she had come upon me when she had. I hoped she hadn't heard me voicing my fears.

If she had heard me, she didn't acknowledge it. "Come," she said. "We must go. I will take you to Eleuterio."

"Why do you call him Eleuterio?" I asked. "He said I could call him Lou."

"I call him Eleuterio out of respect." she said. "It is his name. I have no right to use such a familiar name. He is a great healer and a great teacher. Many have learned from him."

"Lou is easier," I responded. "He said I could call him Lou."

"That is your choice," she said. "You may do as you wish.

"We must go now. It will take several hours to reach Eleuterio."

Though the rain had stopped, the deepening shadows made it difficult to see.

"I don't have a flashlight. Do you?" I asked. "We'll need something."

"No, I do not have a light. I am familiar with the path."

I offered no objection and answered, "Okay."

Christ, I thought. Another adventure. Where was I going ? I was crazy to willingly go into the forest at night, no light, with a stranger, a person from a dream.

Maria motioned for me to follow, and we started down a narrow and barely visible trail. As I walked, I pushed aside bushes and limbs that blocked our path. She stopped and faced me, pulling a branch toward her and stroking the leaves.

"Feel the caress of the branches," she said. "Let them cleanse you. Pull their energy into your body. The plants are powerful healers. Learn from them. Use their power."

She turned and began walking again. Overhead, the clouds were breaking up and I occasionally caught a glimpse of a full moon. Without the moon, I was certain Maria would have been unable to find her way through the hills.

I tried to get her to talk, to tell me more about the plants and Eleuterio, but she gave simple answers or avoided my questions altogether. If she was to help me find my path, I felt she needed to be more responsive.

We had walked for about two hours when she made an abrupt stop. "There is danger ahead," she whispered. "We must be on guard and surround ourselves with protection."

"What kind of danger?" I asked.

"I do not know, but I know we must face the danger without fear. Spirit will protect us. If we allow ourselves to be consumed by our fears, we could perish. Of that I am certain."

"If we encounter danger, how can we stop our fear?" I questioned.

"You must trust Spirit. You will find your strength within. We will proceed with caution." She moved ahead, gliding along the path without making a sound.

I followed close behind, aware that the forest had grown silent. The calls of the night birds and insects had ceased. Fear gnawed at my insides, and I wondered how long the silence had gone unnoticed. Though I attempted to stop it, with each step it grew stronger, and I felt more tension and more fear. I wasn't certain what there was to fear, but Maria had spoken with such seriousness, I was convinced danger was near.

I tried to direct my attention to something else in an effort to calm myself. I thought about the healings I'd seen and wondered how effective the book would be in communicating the message of healing. Though I tried to focus my thoughts upon the book, I was enveloped in an overwhelming sense of dread. Beads of sweat trickled down my forehead. Maria had said to trust Spirit, that we could die if we showed our fear, and wondering what she had meant made me even more fearful.

She reminded me of Lou as she moved through the forest, and I struggled to keep up. Who was she, I wondered. What could I learn from her? I wanted to know her, for she was both beautiful and perceptive, much wiser than her apparent age.

She began running and I fell behind, wondering if she could see in the dark. I called to her, unable to match her pace, and stopped, gasping for breath. She heard my cry and ran back.

"We must not stop," she said. She tugged at my arm. "We are in great danger."

I couldn't move. "I have to rest," I said. "Just give me a couple of minutes."

"Your body is lying," she said. "Do not give in. Show your strength."

As the words left her mouth, four men lunged out of the darkness and pointed automatic weapons at us. One of the men held a light, which he repeatedly moved from me to Maria. Another, a huge Neanderthal looking hulk, grabbed her and pulled out a long, slender knife which he pressed against her throat. He appeared to be nearly seven feet tall.

"What do we have here?" he snarled. "Two lovers hiding in the night?" His voice was deep and resonated through the forest.

"Look," I said. "I only have a little money, but you can have it." I reached into my pocket and held out a few bills.

One of the others, a thin man with a grotesque scar splitting his face diagonally, slammed me across the shoulder with his rifle and grabbed the money as I fell forward. He stared at me with eyes that lacked emotion, narrow slits bisecting his brow.

"Your money is mine and I will take it when I want," Neanderthal growled. He circled the knife around Maria's throat.

"You are so young and pretty. It would be a shame to lose such a beauty, before we have sampled your pleasures. Let us see what the rest of you looks like." With one swift movement, the giant plunged the knife down Maria's shirt, ripping it open.

I lunged at him and was surprised by his quickness. As my fist reached for his jaw, he dodged and struck me in the face with the butt of his knife. The blow knocked me to my knees, and I felt the warm sensation of blood oozing from my forehead.

There was a blur of light and vague figures before me. I turned toward Maria, who formed her lips into a silent, "No." Though she never spoke, I was sure I heard her voice.

"Do not resist. Let go of your fear and your anger. You and I are one with Spirit and will be protected. If we have no fear, we cannot be harmed."

I don't know why, but I grew calm. I pulled myself to my feet, surveying the scene before me. The man with the light shined it upon Maria and stared at her bare breasts. Neanderthal grunted and reached down with his massive hands to touch her, but I'd lost my anger. It was as if I were watching a play—a theatrical, as Mario had called it. The scene wasn't real.

What happened next was incredible. As I watched Neanderthal put his hands on Maria, there was a blinding flash and the giant was thrown ten feet through the air, striking the ground with a dull thud. He lay there, his mouth open as if he wanted to speak, but the only sound he made was a barely audible groan.

The others had watched in anticipation of Neanderthal's actions with Maria and turned their guns toward us in panic. They spoke rapidly with their eyes focused upon her. I was certain they would open fire at any moment. She never spoke and returned their stares with a broad smile. I felt it was impossible, but her body seemed to glow. Then, as quickly as Maria had dispatched Neanderthal, the others threw down their weapons and ran into the forest, abandoning their wounded companion.

"We can go now," Maria said. She spoke as if nothing had happened. "Are you okay?"

She placed her hand on my forehead. In less than a minute the pain was gone.

"Your injury is not serious," she said. "We will soon reach the place where you are to meet Eleuterio and you can rest. We will go now."

With the excitement of our ordeal ended, we both became aware of Maria's torn shirt. I turned away in embarrassment. "I'm sorry," I said.

Maria laughed at my discomfort. She pulled her shirt together, securing it with a strap from a leather bag she carried on her shoulder. "Your embarrassment demonstrates the limits you place upon your world. Do not apologize. It means nothing."

She walked over to the limp body of what, only moments earlier, had been our captor. As she bent down, I noticed how helpless he appeared. He seemed smaller.

She made several sweeping motions around his head, and with each pass seemed to throw some invisible matter to the ground. She continued for three or four minutes, then leaned down and whispered into the giant's ear. When she had finished, she stood and motioned for me to follow her onto the trail.

We hurried through the forest. She moved along as if nothing had happened and never mentioned the strange and dangerous events that had

146

occurred. She seemed indifferent to the experience, her attention focused upon our journey.

We maintained our pace for another hour until we reached a small stream. The surge of adrenaline I'd felt during our ordeal had kept me going, but when we stopped, I collapsed in exhaustion.

"Drink," Maria said. She bent her delicate body to the water.

The water was cool and refreshing. I drank fully and splashed it onto my face.

"We will rest," she said. She leaned against a stone and closed her eyes.

I didn't need to be coaxed and located an area where I could stretch out. As soon as I closed my eyes, I fell into a deep sleep.

During my sleep, I dreamed bizarre dreams. I saw Lou standing over me, with a large knife in his hand. I thought he was going to kill me, but I had no fear. I welcomed death and bent down to accept my fate. My dream faded from view, and I awoke for a few moments.

I fell asleep again and returned to my dream. Again, I experienced the scene with Lou. The dream occurred three times, and each time I seemed eager to accept my fate. Before Lou completed his task, however, I would awaken.

We had slept for a couple of hours when Maria shook me. "We must go," she said. She turned and walked into the forest.

Though I was dazed, I jumped up and followed, shaking my head to clear the clouds from my mind

****

Dawn had come and the sun was high above us before we arrived at a large clearing. Maria opened her bag and offered me a piece of bread similar to the bread that Mario had shared, but hers was filled with nuts and had a slightly sweet taste. I was exhausted and hungry. I devoured it without speaking. When I'd finished, she handed me several narrow strips of dried fruit.

"Eat this," she said.

"What is it?" I asked.

"Mango. It will give you energy."

She pointed to a large pile of stones on the opposite side of the clearing, about a hundred yards away. "Wait there for Eleuterio. He will meet you when the sun passes midday. Beyond the stones you will find a small stream where you can drink."

After our encounter with the bandits, I'd been unable to ask her about what had happened. The pace she'd maintained had kept me gasping for breath, but I was filled with questions. I wanted to know what had happened.

"Tell me what happened with the bandits," I demanded. "What did you do to that giant who was attacking you? It happened so fast I didn't see you touch him."

"I did not touch him," she answered. Her face showed no emotion.

"Well, you did something. You threw him at least ten feet."

"I did not touch him."

"Why won't you explain?" I asked. "Why does everyone talk in riddles and only give minimal information?"

"You saw what your consciousness allows you to accept," she said. "Once it expands allowing you to accept all possibilities, your understanding will be more complete. You are blinded to the truth of your experiences; therefore, I cannot explain it. Let go of your limitations and you will see."

Let go, the phrase everyone used with me. I thought I'd learned to let go.

"It is all very simple," she continued. "Our reality grows out of our experiences, our training. When we are children, our parents, teachers, all those we place in authority, condition our thinking by telling us what can and cannot be; and our minds become corrupted by the narrow vision of reality that is presented. As we grow older, we have our limited view confirmed by others who also were so instructed, and we, unfortunately, reinforce their limitations. We may spend a lifetime in ignorance of both our world and our power, unable to fulfill our destiny of oneness with the Creator."

"How is it possible to overcome our limitations?" I asked. "If we are taught that no other reality exists and we accept such a teaching, how can we see something that, for us, does not exist?"

She looked at me with her beautiful brown eyes, and her words rode on a pathway directed by her vision. My heart seemed to respond to what she said.

"We are given opportunities," she said. "We have choices throughout our lives so that we may experience the other—the real—world. If we ignore our vision, we continue in our blindness, but if we open our hearts for only a brief moment, Spirit guides us to additional insights, expanding our awareness. The choice is ours. Spirit never forces enlightenment upon us.

"Dan, you have seen a small part of the world of Spirit. If you choose to continue, you must be aware and listen in order to recognize the next gift."

"How will I know the next step?" I asked. "How can I be certain the message comes from Spirit?"

Maria looked away as if giving me an opportunity to absorb her words and to find the answers on my own. I wondered how she could be so wise, so full of knowledge. She was so young.

I walked to the stones on the opposite side of the clearing and sat down. I needed to bring order into the confusion I felt.

She spoke as I walked away. "You will know," she said. "You are changing from a caterpillar into a beautiful butterfly. You will know."

How would I recognize the next step? And if I didn't, what would happen then?

I looked toward the trees. Faint sounds, carried by a soft breeze, drifted through the thick growth. The forest seemed to have awareness, feeling. I turned my head and listened. Though I couldn't understand, I felt it was speaking to me.

At the edge of the forest, dozens of beautiful blue butterflies circled round and round. I looked at them in wonder. I'd never before noticed their delicate beauty, the gracefulness they exhibited. I felt connected to them and wished I could share their understanding and their freedom.

As I watched the butterflies, one, larger and more brilliant in color, left the group and began an ever-expanding spiral that brought it closer to where I was seated. I observed the gentle up and down motion of its wings and marveled at its elegance. If only you could speak, I thought. If only I could learn from your connection with Truth. I held out my hand in a gesture of both greeting and supplication.

"Help me," I said. "Help me understand."

As if in response to my plea, the butterfly flew closer and circled my head. Then, in one glorious and uplifting moment, it landed in the palm of my hand!

My body tingled. A wave of emotion and excitement penetrated every cell of my being, and my eyes filled with tears of euphoria. I felt I was experiencing Truth.

Nothing I'd seen, no healing, no materialization, or supernatural event could equal my miracle of Oneness. I was connected with everything, knowing that whatever being, whatever energy filled the universe was speaking to me, and I opened myself in grateful acknowledgment and wonder.

I spoke to the butterfly and watched as it folded and unfolded its fragile wings in reply. I thanked it for hearing me and for responding to my call. I thanked Spirit for sending such a beautiful messenger of love and peace. I was oblivious to my surroundings, to everything. Nothing existed except me and my winged friend. I was in ecstasy.

I'm not certain how long I held the butterfly, but at some point I noticed Maria approaching. As I became aware of her, the butterfly flew up and out of my hand. It circled me several times before rejoining its companions at the edge of the forest.

"Did you see that?" I whispered. "It let me hold it. It spoke to me."

"Yes, Spirit sent the butterfly to help with your awakening. Your chakras are beginning to open. You are very fortunate. You must give thanks and acknowledge your marvelous gift."

"Oh, I did give thanks. It was the most meaningful experience of my life. I hope I can continue to feel so connected."

"Remain open," she instructed. "Do not let your old ways of thinking cloud your vision.

"I must go now." She bent down and kissed me on the cheek. "Eleuterio will be here soon. He will help you. I have enjoyed our adventure. I thank you and I thank Spirit for allowing me to participate in this portion of your journey."

"Will I see you again?" I asked. "I feel there is more you can teach me."

"I do not know. Perhaps we will meet again. Spirit will decide if that is necessary." She began to walk away.

"Maria," I called. I walked over and embraced her. "Thank you for saving my life and for helping me find my path," I said. "If I don't see you again, I wish you well. You are a special person."

"You are special," she said. "You have much more understanding than you imagine."

She turned and walked away without looking back.

I would miss her. Lou was a good teacher, but he wasn't as gentle as Maria and certainly not as beautiful.

I returned to the stone and watched as Maria walked across the clearing, disappearing into the forest. Why couldn't I be as calm, as wise? Why had it taken half my life to reach the point of beginning? I looked down to the stone.

Stone, I thought, even you know more than I. I focused my attention upon the silent and seemingly impenetrable monolith and attempted, as Lou had suggested, to become one with something that only a few months before would have meant nothing. Suddenly, it meant everything, and I struggled to understand, to experience the secrets it held. I stroked its face, worn smooth by centuries of wind and rain.

The stone had patience. There was no urgency to its purpose. It had let go.

CHAPTER 11

THE ENCOUNTER

The cool blackness of the morning
envelops me and calls me to meditation.
I give thanks for the gift of another day.

As my lungs fill with new life,
I quiet my mind and listen to my breath,
aware of sounds, feelings, silence.
The ever-present Now becomes eternity
and I know that life is good.
I am filled with the richness of
experiences untold.

153

I have everything, and
I have nothing.
Life and death are friends,
serenading with their passionate call, yet
neither has more power than the other.
Neither has form or substance.

The silence of the morning calm
will soon be broken
as a new day awakens,
and, once again, I will dance
to the music of life.

While I waited for Eleuterio I tried to meditate like Dr. Won had taught me several months earlier. Although I wasn't meditating daily, as he had suggested, I'd been doing it several times a week, and it seemed to be helping. I felt I'd gained more clarity than before. Maybe I had learned something. But I'd been unable to rid myself of doubt. I wondered if I ever could.

Quieting my mind, sitting in the middle to the jungle, proved to be more difficult than I imagined. I was continually distracted by the sounds, and kept thinking about my predicament. I had no food, no survival gear, and no idea where I was. After a time I gave up.

I glanced at my watch. It was 2:30. I'd been waiting almost four hours. What if there were more bandits? I wondered if it wouldn't have been better if Eleuterio had taken me with him. I silently wished he had.

A knot formed in my stomach and my mouth had the cold metallic taste of fear. Once more I was filled with uncertainties: about the trip, the book, and my life. It seemed crazy that they would resurface so soon. My brief time with Eleuterio had given me strength, helped me lose my fears and doubts. Alone, I lacked both confidence and courage. I knew that if I was ever to be freed from my anxieties, I would have to find my inner resources.

My thoughts were interrupted by a sound coming from the forest. Footsteps. I relaxed and called out. "Over here Lou, by the rocks." There was no reply.

The sound grew louder, closer, and I could hear branches snapping. What if it wasn't Eleuterio? I had stupidly given myself away. I looked around for an escape route or a weapon to defend myself. I couldn't tell where the sound was coming from and reached down, grabbing a softball-sized stone. I stood and braced myself for whatever approached.

I looked towards the dense growth to see an old man stepping into the clearing. His long hair hung down in filthy matted clumps and his clothes were nothing more than tattered rags. He stepped slowly towards me, his eyes darting back and forth like a frightened animal. And he was still more than twenty feet away when his stench reached my nostrils. It was ghastly.

His sudden appearance startled me, and I stared, silently surveying him. I was repulsed by the putrid smell surrounding him. He shuffled to within five feet, watching me through eyes, obscured in a thick milky film. When I backed away he followed, never relinquishing his gaze.

After a few seconds I spoke.

"My name is Dan. Do you speak English? Do you live nearby?"

The old man smiled, revealing a few dark, pointed teeth. I extended my hand, which he encircled with long thin fingers. He had a surprisingly strong grip and pressed his nails into my flesh. I winced in pain, pulling away as he laughed and sprayed me with his foul breath.

"Do you speak English?" I asked again.

"English," he said. His voice was low and raspy and I leaned forward to hear him. "English, yes." His eyes examined me as if he were inspecting livestock, and he took my hands and turned them over exposing my palms. He held them, scrutinizing each line.

155

"I'm here to meet Eleuterio." I jerked out of his grasp. "Do you know him?"

The old man ignored my question and said, "Food. Do you have food?" He spotted a couple of pieces of the dried mango Maria had given me.

Before I could respond, he grabbed the fruit, stuffed it into his mouth, and gulped it down. I looked at him and said. "Have some mango."

"Do you have more?" he asked.

"No, not now."

"Do you know the healer, Eleuterio?" I asked once more.

"Perhaps."

"What do you want?" I asked

"You do not care what I want," he said. "You are afraid of what I may take."

"Look, I'm here to meet my friend. I'm sorry I don't have more food, but I can't help you anymore."

"You have not helped me; I have helped myself."

I slid onto the rock and looked away, hoping he would leave. Instead of leaving, however, he sat down beside me and stared into the forest, appearing to search for whatever he thought I was focused upon. The stench was incredible, and I moved to the edge of the rock, then jumped to the ground. He followed and stood beside me.

"What do you want?" I said.

"What do you want?" he whispered.

"You wouldn't understand," I responded. I thought how silly it seemed, trying to communicate with him. He was getting on my nerves. I coughed and turned away.

"Don't like my perfume?" He looked at me and sneered. "Don't like yours either."

The situation was growing more ridiculous with each moment. "Old man," I said. "I don't know who you are—"

"And do not care, do you?" he interrupted.

"I don't know what you want," I said. "I don't have any more food. I'm here to meet a friend. I can't help you."

"I did not ask for your help," he said. "But I can give help to you. I know the answers to your questions. I know what you want."

"You have no idea what I want," I said

"I can save you much time and effort. You have many questions. I have many answers."

"Okay," I said. I thought perhaps I could pacify him. If I played his game, he might leave.

"Why am I here?" I asked.

"I can surely tell you, but first you must pay."

"Now I understand, you want money. Well, I don't have any, so you're out of luck. If you have all the answers, you should know I have no money. Tell me why I'm here. Where did I come from?"

"America. You come from America."

"I don't think you'd win a prize for that answer," I said. "Most anyone could guess that."

"Perhaps," he said. "And perhaps they would know your innermost secret as I do."

"I don't know what you want, and I told you I have no money. Maybe you should look for someone else to help you."

"I do not need help. As you see I can help myself, but I think you would like to know what I can tell you. First you must pay."

"How can I pay you? Don't you understand I have no money?"

"Airplanes cost money. You came here in an airplane. And you have other things too. Tell me about your boat."

"How do you know that? How do you know I have a boat? Who are you?"

"Now you have interest. Maybe now you will pay."

"Who are you? Did Eleuterio send you? What did he tell you?" I relaxed, realizing the old man must be another of Lou's tricks. I wondered why he had sent him.

"What am I supposed to do?" I asked.

"I care not. Do what you wish. But if you want answers, you must pay."

I sat down on the rock and tried to ignore the man, hoping Eleuterio would show up. If there was a purpose to our encounter, I assumed I wouldn't need to search for it. The old man sat next to me, his shoulder rubbing mine. I was glad I had a strong stomach. He pulled his knees to his chest and leaned his head forward. His breathing was slow and rhythmic.

"Relax," he whispered. "You should learn to relax."

"I can relax. I've been meditating for two hours."

"Can not see it in your eyes. You are filled with stress and fear. You are uncomfortable in my forest. Why do you frighten so easily?

I didn't know how to respond and closed my eyes. I wasn't learning anything from him, and wasn't sure I could.

I must have dozed off and awoke with a start when I thought I heard Lou's voice. I looked up, expecting to see him walking across the clearing, but he wasn't there. And the old man was gone too. I wondered how he had been able to slip away without waking me.

He had said he knew the answers to my questions. That seemed doubtful. There was probably little he knew in which I'd be interested. And since he had gone without telling me anything, I began to doubt if he had been sent by Lou. But how had he known about the boat? Maybe he had some psychic ability or maybe he just assumed I owned a boat because I'm an American. It didn't matter. He was gone, and once more I was alone, searching for answers.

Though I'd found some relief from my frustrations, I knew I was far from where I needed to be. I wondered if Lou would be able to help me resolve the many issues that troubled me. Perhaps my expectations were unrealistic, but I needed to be sure. I had to give him the opportunity. Most of all I hoped he could help me find peace.

As I reflected I heard a familiar voice. "Hello, my friend." I turned to see Lou coming across the clearing. "I see that Maria delivered you to our rendezvous."

I stood and walked out to meet him. "Where have you been?" I asked. "While I was waiting an old man came here. He seemed rather mysterious, told me he could answer my questions, and I thought you might have sent him. But when he asked for money, I realized he was only a beggar."

Eleuterio stopped and turned to me. "What did this man look like? Tell me exactly what he said."

I described the old man and told Lou as much as I remembered of our conversation. He listened without speaking, then furrowed his brow.

"I think you have met a messenger from the other side," he said. "If so, he did not want money. Did you ask what sort of payment he desired?"

159

"He looked pathetic. I assumed he wanted money. Why didn't he tell me he wanted something else?"

"Did you ask?"

"No. You should have warned me that I might meet someone like him."

"This is very unusual. I have not had such an encounter in many years. It is not good that you sent him away."

Lou shook his head. "Your actions may have cost you an opportunity to step into the next realm, a tragedy beyond your understanding. Open your eyes! How can you expect to gain wisdom, if you will not see what is before you?"

"I'm sorry," I said. "I had a conversation with an old man, but it seemed to have no significance. How can I see beyond what I know?"

"You know nothing for you refuse to listen. Spirit provides you with opportunities and you ignore them. You make no attempt to see beyond the veil of illusion. Everything in your experience is of Spirit and has meaning. Your blindness may have created additional obstacles to your journey."

Lou pointed to the rocks where I'd waited earlier. "Sit and tell me everything that occurred after I left you in my house. I must know every detail."

I described how I had awakened, discovering him gone, how I'd stepped outside and seen Maria, and the long trek we made through the forest. "Late last evening, around midnight, we were attacked by bandits, and Maria used your force or something to allow us to escape. It was incredible. How did she do it? Is it something you could teach me?"

"I am not certain you can learn," he said. "Such manifestations of Spirit are the result of an inward condition of Oneness. Only after reaching such a condition will you understand. You must open yourself to the messages from Spirit."

"My problem is," I said. "I don't know where or how to begin. I've read books and been to classes, but I'm no further along in my spiritual development than when I began. I need specifics. What can I do?"

"The spiritual path is difficult and is filled with many obstacles. I will try to help you recognize your path. Sometimes that can be enough.

"Remember," he said, "Our world is a world of vibration. Everything from the smallest grain of sand to the highest mountain is vibration, energy, and that includes us humans. If you can understand and accept that your body is the same as the mountain, you will see how the connection between the two allows for your so-called miracles to occur.

"One way to begin listening, to gain understanding, is through meditation. Meditation clears the mind and makes way for enlightenment. As regular exercise strengthens the physical body, a practice of meditation will increase one's spiritual awareness."

"I've tried it," I said. "I learned a meditation technique when I was in Arizona. Sure it helps me reach a more peaceful state, but I don't get messages from God. I don't get messages from anyone. How can it be something else, something more?"

"What you have practiced is exactly as you describe," he said. "It is for relaxation. The form I propose, will allow you to contact your higher self, which is Spirit."

"That's my problem," I said. "What do I do in order to contact this higher self? I've never felt I was even close."

"You have an expectation of what meditation will accomplish. Release that vision and allow yourself to be engulfed in the wonder and

161

mystery of Spirit. You must maintain your belief that enlightenment will come.

"Your success is dependent upon your willingness to commit to a daily ritual of meditation. Have patience. It could take months, perhaps years, to achieve the state you desire, but your time will be spent wisely. Few are willing to dedicate themselves to this practice; most abandon their efforts, frustrated by their lack of immediate success. And the tragic element of their failure is that the perceived sacrifice is only illusion."

"Is it really possible for someone like me to do it?" I asked. "You wouldn't believe the number of books, workshops, and classes I've seen that teach meditation. Millions have tried it, yet almost no one reaches the state you describe."

"Meditation is a paradox. In order to meditate, it is not necessary to focus your thoughts upon a thing, for you are not trying to accomplish something. There is no objective, yet the rewards are beyond description. Yes, you are to relax, but you must let your mind do as it pleases. There must be no effort. To exert effort is to defeat the purpose of the meditation."

"How do I do that?" I asked. "Where do I start?"

"The way to remove your distractions," he said, "is with the breath. Breath is the key to life and is alive with prana. When you begin your meditation, start with slow, deep, measured breaths. Your breath is much more than a method of circulating air through your lungs. It brings in prana, the energy of life. It must penetrate every cell of your body."

"I've taken yoga classes," I said. "And I've studied deep breathing. It never got me anywhere. What's different about your method?"

"Dan, have you forgotten all that you have seen and experienced? How many of those past teachers could close a wound, could let you visit your past, and help you see your true self? Do you not understand that I

162

might know a better way? The path I show you is the path to wisdom, healing, and Oneness. Be patient, listen, and you will change your life."

Lou instructed me sit on the ground. As I sat down he had me raise my right hand, holding my palm towards him. He squatted about ten feet away and began to point the index and middle fingers of his right hand toward my outstretched palm. He rotated his fingers, drawing an invisible circle.

"Close your eyes," he said. "Concentrate on your palm. Think of nothing but your palm."

I closed my eyes as he instructed and began to focus my attention on my hand. I wondered what he was doing.

It took less than a minute for me to find out. First, my palm began to tingle in a circular pattern that simulated the motion of his fingers. A few seconds more and it began to get warm, then hot. Moments later my hand felt like it was on fire, as if I were holding hot coals.

I dropped my hand and opened my eyes. "How did you do that?" I asked. My palm burned and had turned deep red.

He walked over and made a few motions over my hand similar to the ones Maria had done with Neanderthal. My hand instantly felt cool and the color returned to normal.

"I sent my energy to your hand," Lou said. "By concentrating on that small area, I was able to focus a great amount of energy. That is what I learned from meditation. If I can change the energy in your hand in such a way, then I can also use that power for good—for healing."

"Okay," I said. "Show me your way. I want to learn."

"Good. We can begin."

CHAPTER 12

INITIATION

Lou led me deep into the forest, into an area he described as a "power center." There was a small hut that could barely accommodate the two of us, but we stayed there for more than a week. We had no food except for some hard bread that we shared in a single midday meal. Nearby, a beautiful stream provided us with the sweetest water I've ever tasted. According to Lou, the spring brought forth water from the center of the earth and had been there since the beginning of time.

We spent the remainder of that day in what I can only describe as prayer, but it was unlike any prayer I'd ever observed. Lou said I must be properly focused in order to receive the training that was about to begin, yet he did all of the praying; and his prayers were little more than barely audible phrases.

During his prayers, he occasionally pressed his fingers into my temples, stared into my eyes, and chastised me for past behaviors. He wasn't criticizing me for my actions though. He seemed to be showing me how I'd not been open to the opportunities for spiritual growth that such events presented. It was incredible how much of my past he saw. He caused me to recall events, beginning in early childhood, memories that had been long forgotten. Yet, as he described an event, I was drawn into it with such intensity that I re-experienced sounds, smells, and emotions that made it seem I was actually there.

Lou had me examine each vision, instructing me to focus upon the meaning it held for me. Sometimes I received only a single word or feeling, but I began to see how each occurrence, each action, presented unique opportunities for growth. My outward reaction to those incidents had not been the critical issue, only whether or not I had grown.

Seeing those missed opportunities, I felt remorse, and more than once I choked with emotion. But there were also moments of extraordinary peace and serenity as I saw how the prospect for change still existed.

As the sun melted into the horizon, ending my first day, I was exhausted. I was pleased when Lou invited me into the hut where I collapsed onto a mat, immediately falling into a dreamless sleep.

The next morning I awoke to the sound of an eerie cry coming from outside the hut. Once again, I was reminded of the strange bird that had circled Conquest. I raised my head and noticed, with surprise, that Lou's mat was undisturbed, and he was nowhere in sight. After several more of the strange cries, I called out for him.

The only response was a continuation of the cries, which, it seemed, were being answered from within the forest.

I checked the time. It was 5:30 A.M. In the growing light, I could just make out the outline of a man—I hoped it was Lou—sitting in front of a small fire.

"Lou," I called again. "Did you hear that sound? I've heard that same shrill cry several times. I heard it the morning you—or whatever I experienced as you—appeared on my boat. After I heard the call, a giant bird circled overhead. What does it mean?"

The figure turned to face me, and I was relieved to hear Lou's familiar voice. "It is said that there are people who can transform themselves into animals. Do you believe that is possible?"

"At this point, I'm not sure what I believe," I said. "But I'm probably not ready to accept the concept of men changing into animals. Sounds too much like science fiction."

"Yes, you are not ready to believe. That is the core of your problem. You will never understand until you believe. Do not place limits on what can or cannot be. Spirit knows no such limits."

"Tell me what I heard. What was it?"

"I was calling to the forest to ask for guidance as we begin your lessons. The sounds you heard were the sounds of Spirit speaking through the voice of the trees. You are fortunate, for Spirit has shown me the path for your awakening."

"Wait a minute," I said. "Were you making the bird sound? Are you saying you can transform yourself into a bird, that it was you I saw circling my boat?"

"No, I did not say that. Whatever you saw was your vision and is unimportant to me."

Lou pointed to the trees. "Our friends have spoken. Come. We will go into the forest. You are filled with the chaff of many lifetimes of false thinking. You need a catalyst to open your mind to the knowledge and wisdom of Spirit."

He reached to his side and pulled out a long knife, its bright steel glistening in the firelight.

"I will open a hole in your skull to allow the waste to escape and the bounty of Spirit to flow in. You need a surgical remedy."

I wanted to know more about the bird and whether or not Lou was involved, but his words caused me to twitch in fear of what he might have in mind. "What do you mean?" I asked.

"It is simple. I will make a hole in your skull."

"No, what do you really mean? Obviously, I'm not to take you literally, for I would die."

"Yes, you may die." he said. "But you were ready to give up your life only a short time ago, and it seems to me that your present life has not changed very much. I cannot see why you would want to keep it."

"Do you mean psychic surgery," I asked. "Is that what you're going to do?"

"No, that method does not hold the power to correct your condition. You need the most forceful procedure possible. You need an opening in your skull."

My body trembled as a vision filled my mind. I stared beyond Lou into a scene of pure terror, a vision of him standing over me, pulling huge masses of horrible slime from my skull. I remembered the dream I'd had.

"That's not funny," I said. My voice was barely a whisper. "Tell me what you mean."

"I mean exactly what I said, nothing more or less. You will soon understand, and the pain you may feel will be a small price to pay for such a great reward. I have only begun to realize how poisoned you are. It will take all of the power I can summon to remove this poison from your system. The gates to your true self have become frozen by the rust of your sordid accumulation of material objects. You have forgotten your purpose.

"If you were to die this very day," he continued. "What event, what contribution to your Earth Mother could you point out as your legacy to mankind? Your life has been lived in selfish disregard for the earth and for others. You, and millions like you, have destroyed our forests, poisoned our air and water, and killed entire species of plants and animals. Your gluttony creates a cloud that fills my nostrils with the stench of death, and your futile attempts to correct these problems would be humorous if the results were not so lethal."

Lou held the knife before me once more. "As you reflect on my words you will feel the pain of your ignorance. Perhaps you may someday share your pain and your understanding with others who are ready to hear. If only a few become sensitive to our struggle for survival, we may be able to reverse our march toward extinction.

"It is time to prepare for your awakening."

He turned and walked into a small opening at the edge of the clearing. I only hesitated a moment before following him into the thick underbrush.

We didn't speak and walked briskly in the pale orange light of the emerging dawn. Occasionally, Lou paused and appeared to pick up something as his hand swept along the ground and quickly moved to a small leather pouch hanging from his belt. The speed of his movements and the shadows of the forest concealed whatever he was gathering. I was curious, but felt I shouldn't question him. Instead, my mind ran a moving picture of the potential danger I faced. Though I was frightened, I wanted to know more about what he planned.

After about an hour of his gathering, we returned to the clearing. He instructed me to put wood on the fire. As I did, he opened his pouch and poured out a number of small mushrooms, which he examined, one by one. He mumbled as he scrutinized each one, separating them into two groups. The larger group, consisting of about twenty, dark brown mushrooms with unusually small caps, was placed on a flat stone at his side.

He took another stone and began pounding the mushrooms until they were pulverized into a powdery mass. I watched as he emptied about half of the water from his canteen and, using his knife, carefully scraped the mushroom powder into the container. As soon as it was filled, he replaced the cap and put the canteen in the center of the fire, supporting it with two small stones.

It's going to blow, I thought, staring at the canteen, its cap securely in place. I slid, as far as my rock would allow, away from the impending explosion and tensed in anticipation. However, I watched with surprise as a small geyser of steam spewed from a tiny hole in the center of the cap.

"We must cook the 'little flowers' to prepare for your surgery." Lou looked up at me with a slight smile. "I have thanked them for coming to assist your awakening. You will sit without speaking as I prepare myself and our friends for this work."

"I'm not sure I'm ready for this," I said. I stood and looked around. "What are you going to do?"

"No, you are not ready for this, but you cannot wait. Your instruction must begin now. We will have to deal with the risks of beginning too soon. Sit."

I had become accustomed to the strange power he seemed to have over me, and sat without speaking. Lou turned towards the fire and began to sway and sing in an unintelligible language. He sang softly at first, but as the fire slowly began to change into a glowing mass of coals, his voice rose until it caused me to vibrate within. It seemed as if his words were being sung inside me. I could almost feel my body singing in unison.

Little more than an hour had passed when Lou grabbed a stick and pulled the canteen from the remains of the fire. He scooped out a small depression in the soil and gently eased the canteen in, covering the exposed portion with damp leaves that sizzled as they made contact. He was still swaying, but his singing had stopped, replaced by a low, moaning sound.

A half hour later Lou took the container and poured a couple of ounces of dark brown syrup into a small cup. He held the cup in front of him.

"This is usually taken after sundown," he said. "But the 'little flowers' tell me I must not waste time in preparing for your awakening. They are ready to do their work." He took his knife and stepped over to where I was seated.

If I am to die, I thought, I'm ready. I no longer feared the events for which he had prepared and looked up at him. I closed my eyes in anticipation of what was to come.

I waited. Nothing happened! I opened my eyes to see Lou cutting a small reed and placing it in the cup.

"Drink," he said. He thrust the cup into my hand. "Drink through the reed. It will not come easily, but suck with all your might and drink it all. You are ready. Drink."

I took the cup and sucked on the reed; grateful I didn't have blood running down my forehead. My gratitude disappeared, though, as I became aware of the fowl tasting brew filling my mouth, and I had to fight to keep from throwing up. The stuff was awful.

"Drink all of it," Lou insisted.

It was difficult keeping it down, and I swallowed hard, consuming the remaining portion in one final gulp. I'd never tasted anything like it.

"Here, drink this." He handed me another cup.

"What is it," I asked.

"Drink it," he said. "This will remove some of the bitter taste and will help the little flowers do their work. Sit quietly and allow the work to begin."

The drink in the second cup did remove the bitterness, but burned my throat as it quickly made its way to my stomach. I put down the cup and stared into the remains of the fire, by that time nothing more than a few coals with a pulsating glow. As I gazed at the coals, they seemed to be aware of my presence. I swayed in rhythm with their pulse. My swaying continued for a few minutes, and I looked up, first at Lou, then into the surrounding forest. The trees were vibrating in unison with my movements, and I could see beyond the huge trunks, limbs, and leaves into the hearts of the trees themselves. They had life, the same kind of life that I had!

Never before had I experienced such a sensation, a total connection with something that, for me, had no consciousness. I was fascinated by my discovery and was drawn to the trees, wanting them to know I understood. I was one of them. I stood and walked toward a group of trees about twenty feet away. As I neared, I was sucked into the heart of a giant mahogany that stood apart from the others. I was inside the tree!

My rational self told me that the experience could not be, that it was some sort of hallucination, but the argument was not convincing. I could feel the warmth of the wet, sticky sap coursing around my body, the movement of the tree as it breathed.

As I analyzed what was happening, I grew frightened. Was I losing my mind or was the experience somehow real, part of a different dimension of which I was unaware? Neither alternative assuaged my fear, and I attempted to slow down my sensory input in order to survey my situation

The experience did not subside, intensifying as I moved upwards through the massive trunk, following the flow of the tree's life fluid. I was pulled up and out into the huge limbs, towering over the forest, viewing the world as a tree does. Though I can't explain it, I experienced the sensations of the tree, no longer separate from the forest giant, but connected in a manner I can't describe.

I felt the warmth of the earth below as the roots searched the soil for moisture, and it all made sense. I wasn't separate from any form of life. I was all life and all life was within me. In one moment I knew that my vision, my understanding would never again be limited by my experience as a single and separate entity. The sensation was overwhelming.

Without warning, the tree spoke. I didn't just perceive its consciousness; some previously unknown sensory faculty heard it speak. The sensations, the emotions that were conveyed allowed me to see and experience life as a tree does. I was given a vision from the consciousness, the memory of the tree that filled me with sorrow.

I felt the earth tremble as huge steel monsters, engulfed in the acrid smell of diesel fuel, trampled ancient forests that had once been the habitat of thousands of life forms. I heard the cries of centuries old trees as giant and vicious saws tore into their flesh. The trees were frightened of man, but felt compassion as they observed man's ignorant disregard for the sanctity of life.

My journey spanned centuries, and I saw how man had once been conscious of his connection with other forms of life, how he had long ago lost his awareness, now viewing such thinking as primitive. I was shown that all life—trees, plants, animals, and man—is sacred. One form has no more significance than another. To elevate myself was pure arrogance.

It seemed so simple, so natural, but the experience was, for me, an astounding revelation. I had perceived life in a manner never before experienced and could no longer ignore the unity of all things. I was transformed.

Although my experience caused me to lose my sense of time, at some point I became aware that I needed to return to my human experience. In an instant I found myself on the stone where I'd been seated. Lou was there and placed his fingertips on my forehead.

"You have visited with our forest friends," he said. "That is good. They have a way of expression I cannot duplicate. They are much wiser that I."

"Lou, it was incredible. How did you know?"

"Spirit showed me the way for your awakening. The little flowers were the tools to open your mind. The difficulty for you will be in preserving your understanding, for the poisons in your mind are strong and cannot easily be dissolved."

"When I'm here with you, it all seems so natural, as if I always had this knowledge," I responded.

"Yes, but you will not always have this environment in which to join with Spirit. In a few days you must return to your home. I will try to show your how to remain connected so that you may continue to develop your new awareness."

CHAPTER 13

THE LESSONS

Each day thereafter we arose at 5:00 A.M. and meditated for two hours. We began our meditations with a series of breathing exercises that Lou said removed the debris from both my body and my mind.

"Proper breathing quiets the mind," he said. You must inhale through your nose and exhale through your mouth. As you exhale, allow your breath to make a quiet *shhh* sound. Breathe deeply into the pit of your stomach, expanding your diaphragm and sending the energy of breath into all parts of your body.

"Then," he continued, "as the meditation begins, you should not hear your breath. Breathe in a quiet, slow, and rhythmic fashion, and you will experience the calmness that is necessary for meditation."

After the breathing exercises, I allowed my breath to find its proper rhythm. "Do not try to regulate your breath," he said. "You will be distracted. Your body will set the breathing pattern it needs."

"Do not be concerned with thoughts that arise in your mind," he instructed. "Observe them and let them pass. After a time, your mind will quiet itself, and as you practice, you will find you can reach a state of quietness more quickly."

The meditations were wonderful. Never before had I experienced such a sense of pure contentment. My understanding of the world, of life, began to change, and I saw a portion of the other realities that both Mario and Lou had alluded to.

I once read that words are twice removed from reality, and, at the time, the meaning wasn't quite clear to me. Through my meditations, however, I saw and understood exactly what the writer had meant. Words can't describe the infinite. I finally knew why Lou had been unable to tell me what he experienced. Such experiences are impossible to communicate to others.

Rationalizing the things I saw was difficult, because I couldn't quantify my experiences. My thoughts were limited to words, but the workings of Spirit or God, whatever we call it, transcend language. Such can be known but not expressed.

As I practiced my meditations, I began to see how my past had been a necessary part of my growth. The parts of my life I'd previously condemned had helped me reach my present position. Each trauma, each experience, whether seen as good or bad, became a stone in the foundation of my life. I could look to the future with anticipation, content in the knowledge that each event would serve to bring me one step closer to my ultimate goal of Oneness.

After our meditations, Lou began my training. He showed me how to feel the energy of others and how to detect the subtle differences that accompany disease. He would alter his energy field, his prana, to duplicate that of a sick person, allowing me to feel the differences. I saw his energy and watched in amazement as it changed before me. He taught me how to sensitize my hands so that I might feel the powerful energy that surrounds us all.

At times Lou would go into long discourses about the energy that is life. Resting on the large boulders lining the edge of the stream, he would sit cross-legged, his back erect, talking for hours without moving. I was too stiff for that position and faced him with my back resting against the stone wall that rose from the side of the stream.

"Everyone has prana," he said. "The energy surrounds and interpenetrates their physical body and can be seen by those who are sensitive to it. However, for many, it is easier to feel than to see the energy. Prana is often referred to as the aura and can extend from several inches to two feet or more from the body.

"Unfortunately, there is much confusion about the energy body, and the confusion has caused it to be ignored by most of the scientific community. With a little practice, however, anyone can learn to feel the energy and sometimes see its physical manifestation."

Lou was providing concrete information that made sense. I wondered if I would gain understanding of the other realities I'd experienced.

He continued, "An important aspect of the energy body is the location of the chakras. The chakras are the centers that serve to energize the major organs and functions of the physical body. When the chakras are functioning properly, they serve to distribute prana throughout the body in accordance with its needs. Malfunctioning chakras cause disease to be expressed in the physical."

"I've read about the chakras," I said. "Aren't they responsible for psychic powers?"

"Yes, some of them are centers for psychic development. The solar plexus and the head are the location of major chakras that can be utilized to expand one's psychic abilities. The hands are the location of one the minor chakras, and, as you have experienced, can be utilized to perceive the energy body and determine if disease is present.

"When you use this knowledge for healing," he said, "remember that the condition expressed as illness, only exists in illusion. What appears as disease or disharmony is only the misguided thought that a condition exists apart from Spirit. That, of course, cannot be. To remove disease you must remove the illusion. Your understanding will tell you that the person is perfect and only fails to recognize their perfection. Use that knowledge to create an illusion of health. Once the person accepts their new illusion, it becomes reality and they are healed.

"It is simple," he said. "It is so simple that most people find it difficult to accept. That is why you, and others like you, are so important. Without the few who transcend the world of illusion, our world would be lost."

It was difficult to accept the illusion part. Sure, it made sense, but applying it to my life, actually living it, was much harder than I imagined.

Lou demonstrated the various techniques he used to remove disease and showed me how to energize a person after the disease had been removed. He taught me how to draw prana from the air, from trees, and from the ground.

"If you use only your own prana for healing, you will quickly become depleted," he said. " Neither you nor the sufferer will benefit. The energy for healing is in everything around you. Draw upon these sources and you will always have sufficient for your needs."

He spent hours discussing how I could utilize my new awareness to bring healing to myself, to others, and to the world. I asked for clarification. "When I'm trying to heal someone, do I focus my attention on the person as a whole or only on the specific area to be healed?"

Lou looked at me and laughed. "Do not try. Heal. Do not think. Be. You are the universe. You are the healer and the person to be healed. What could I tell you to think on that you do not already know? You are one with all things. Feel your Oneness. That is what you should do."

"I'm confused about why I need to perform healing. If the world is perfect, what difference does it make if I heal or not?"

"The purpose for healing is not the removal of a condition," he answered. "Your intent is the realization of Oneness and is necessary for both the healer and the person to be healed. Each time you perform healing, you are expressing your Oneness, allowing it to be shared by others. Healing is necessary because of the perfection of the world, not because the world is imperfect.

"Man dreams he is lost, but it is only within his dream that he is lost. He has lost his awareness of his true self. Our healings sometimes

179

awaken man from his dream, and once awakened, he may awaken others. One day, perhaps, all will experience reunion with Spirit."

We discussed prayer and man's continual struggle to communicate with a higher power. "Most prayer is a meaningless and non-productive form of begging," he said. "Man's very limited view places his god in the position of either a servant, awaiting man's command, or a ruthless despot who seems to delight in the sufferings of his subjects."

He raised his arms toward the sky. "We don't need to remind Spirit that we are suffering or in need. God would not be God without awareness of all conditions. If we ask Him to eliminate a condition, we see Him as a means to an end, and the only end worthy of our desires is the realization of Oneness."

"Are you saying that there is no reason to use prayer as I know it?" I asked. "What about the churches, the people who are healed when others pray for them?"

"People are healed because they release their illusion of disease," he answered. "It is often possible for those who have no understanding of Spirit to help others change their beliefs. Acceptance of the illusion, regardless of the source, always causes the body to respond accordingly. That is the reason such prayers often work. But you find many more instances where prayer is unsuccessful, do you not? In those cases, the sick, their friends and families, may be confused by the apparent lack of response from God. Those in religion may place the responsibility upon to the diseased person for their lack of faith. However, it is not a lack of faith, but a lack of understanding that fails to bring about healing."

One morning, Lou taught me how to redirect the energy of an opponent and how to return it with even greater force than when it was sent. That, he explained, is what Maria had done with the giant who was molesting her. The others had fled because Maria had released her physical body, allowing her energy body to become visible. Apparently, I had seen her glowing!

"One should not have to use the energy for self-defense, except in the most rare occasions," he explained. "If your life is in harmony with Spirit, no ill can befall you."

"I wish I had your wisdom," I said. "It seems so easy for you. You have a level of understanding I'm not sure I can ever reach. I don't understand why some people, the so-called adepts who have existed throughout time, seem to have no difficulty in grasping he infinite. Why couldn't I have been born with such wisdom?"

"You were," he responded. He looked at me and frowned. "I am no different from you or from anyone else. Yes, I have understanding, more perhaps than some others, but the understanding is there for everyone. The difference is: I listen."

"That's what I'm talking about," I said. "What made you listen? What allowed you to accept a world that is so different from mine? I, and millions like me, have searched for meaning. We would have listened to a higher power if we were aware It was speaking to us. Why is it so obvious to you and so obscure to the rest of the world?"

"No, you have not listened," he chided. "Your heart has been closed to the wisdom of Spirit. Your materialistic life has created distractions that kept you from listening. You expected Spirit to speak within the framework of your limited view. You were not open. Your attempts to direct Spirit have caused you to ignore the path that opened before you.

"However, it does not matter that you once failed to listen," he continued. "What is important is that you are now ready to accept."

"What about the others?" I asked. "I feel fortunate I was able to meet you and have you as my teacher. What about all those who never find a teacher to assist in their search. It doesn't seem fair."

"It is not fair and should not be. That is the way of life. Your concept of fairness cannot be applied in a comparison with the life of another for you cannot know what path another has chosen. Do not concern yourself with what is or is not fair. You will understand when you discover your true identity."

"But what about finding a teacher?" I asked. "Isn't it easier to learn if one has someone to show the way, someone who has already been there?"

"Finding a teacher is unimportant. Each person, each soul, is on a journey of learning and discovery. We will encounter a teacher if it is appropriate for us to do so, but it is possible and sometimes easier, to learn from our experiences. Teachers may remove the barriers that blind us to our lessons, but you must know that you could have done the same without assistance from others. You summon a teacher when your higher self feels it necessary. Teachers never appear by chance.

"Your task is to remain open to the lessons that Spirit presents. Ultimately, it is you who has set up the events of your life, and with the guidance of Spirit, you will discover your path and will have the strength and courage to follow it."

"I don't understand," I said. "I didn't call you into my life. I didn't know you existed, and I certainly wasn't searching for truth."

Lou hesitated as he pondered my remarks. "Dan," he said. "Your conscious self is unaware of the movements of Spirit, for your mind cannot accept those things that are beyond the physical. That is the function of intuition. I cannot explain the workings of Spirit, for it is impossible to put into words the concepts and purpose of a force far greater than the human mind can imagine. It is like the force of electricity. I can show you a wire that contains sufficient voltage to kill you, but the wire itself, appears harmless. The force is there, but it cannot be detected through simple observation. Your past experiences may convince you that the power is present, and you may utilize the power to accomplish many things. Ultimately, you must demonstrate your trust, your faith in this great, unseen force.

"You cannot comprehend the existence of the unlimited power of Spirit, yet you see the results each day. In order for you to reach your goal of Oneness, you must continue your journey with the awareness that you and Spirit are one."

Maybe I wasn't getting it. Acceptance of the working of Spirit in all areas of my life seemed an impossible task. I needed tangible evidence as a starting point upon which to build belief. I couldn't just accept things blindly.

"Have patience," Lou said. "If you attune yourself to Spirit—if you listen—you will achieve understanding, an understanding I cannot explain. You will know which path to follow. You will feel your Oneness without the need of a teacher to guide you. You become the teacher."

"Why does it take so long?" I asked. "I've been in darkness all my life."

"You think in terms of illusion," he said. "Time does not exist. The world of the physical is here for your learning, for your growth, and the results are measured by your acceptance of your connection to all things. What you call pain and suffering are parts of your growth, parts of a divine plan. Every minute, every experience of your life is an element of that plan and is sacred. You have selected your experiences. Reflect upon them with the understanding that they are assisting in your return to your true self."

Lou's words were a healing salve to the open wounds of my psyche. Maybe I could understand. If only I could maintain my level of awareness once I returned to my other life.

"What can I do?" I asked. "How can I keep from losing this feeling, this understanding, when I return to Boston?"

"Do nothing," he said. "You have awakened to Spirit and that cannot be forgotten. But you must not abandon your old life, for you have work to do. You cannot remove yourself from your past. Accept your new awareness. You will view things differently, and you will be seen by your friends and associates as having experienced a great change. Listen to your inner voice. You will be led in directions you never dreamed possible."

"That's one of the things that bothers me," I said. "I want to do the things that will keep me on my path, and I'm interested in helping my fellow man. But a healer? I just don't see it. It doesn't seem like me."

"I did not instruct you to begin a healing practice." he responded. "There are many paths for us to follow. Healing is but one."

"But you've placed so much emphasis upon healing and taught me many healing techniques. I feel obligated to use the knowledge. After all, there is a lot of sickness in the world."

Lou smiled as one might to a child. He bent down to pick up a small stone. "This stone is one of millions, each important in its own way. Healing is the same. It is but a small element in the portrait of life. As an artist covers a canvas with many colors, you will also use many things you have learned—and things yet to be learned—in your portrait of life. Knowledge of healing will keep your body in proper condition, for there may be times you will need extraordinary strength and endurance."

I shuddered, wondering what he had in mind.

****

By the tenth day, I sensed subtle changes taking place in my awareness. The time had come for me to leave. Though I didn't feel I was ready, I wanted to apply the lessons I'd learned into the realm I'd mistakenly referred to as the "real world." I could see how wrong that description had been.

A new life was opening before me, changing in ways I could never have imagined. The things Lou had shown me were easier to accept and, although I lacked a complete understanding, I felt I had caught a glimpse of God. My consciousness had expanded to allow for a new paradigm, and my old concepts were no longer useful in examining a new and fascinating reality.

However, I could see how little I actually understood. I had more questions than ever. I hoped my understanding would continue to evolve and would never again allow me to slip into the despair that had once been an integral part of my life.

Thoughts of returning to Boston made me apprehensive. In Lou's presence I'd felt secure, able to view my problems with a different perspective. His superior perception seemed to have improved my ability to perceive. I hoped it would last. Though I wasn't certain what the future held, I knew I could remain with him no longer.

He sensed my anxiety and tried to calm my fears. "You have begun to see your truth. Return to America. Use your knowledge to assist your friend Mike and allow your awakened consciousness to expand. There is much to learn. Trust Spirit to lead you. Listen."

CHAPTER 14

THE FOUNDATIONS
OF TRUTH

Early the next morning, Lou led me through the forest to the village where he had treated the injured family during my first visit to the Philippines. He told me Andres' would drive me to Manila.

"You are fortunate, for Andres' recently received the automobile of his deceased father. Without that you might have waited until Mario could purchase another. Spirit has delivered a way to meet your needs."

Andres' walked up and greeted us. He spoke to Lou, then backed away.

Lou turned to me. "You must go quickly," he said. "The automobile has no headlights and is not safe to be driven after dark. I have told Andres' the route you must take and I have drawn him a crude map. I think he understands, but you may need to help him."

"Before I leave," I said. "I have one question . . . a very important question I must ask."

"Yes," Lou answered. "What is your very important question."

"You've taught me a great deal," I said. " I appreciate your time and your patience, but there's something I still don't understand."

I paused, making one last attempt to understand on my own.

"Tell me," I said. "Did you come to Boston last March? Was it you that came to my boat?"

Andres' said something to Lou and made a nervous gesture toward the car.

Lou turned and spoke, "Andres' says you must go now. You cannot keep him waiting. It is, as we say, *utang na loob*, a debt of gratitude. It is remarkable that he is willing to take you, for he has never driven to Manila. He has never driven outside of this province, but he feels the responsibility of his debt and does it for me. You must not delay him. He is fearful of this trip."

"I have to know. Was it you?"

"Yes." He seemed annoyed. "You saw me, but I was not there. I cannot explain. You are not yet ready for the answer. You must go."

"I'm sorry, I appreciate Andres' concerns, but I have to know more. Tell me something that will help me understand," I pleaded.

187

Lou looked at me, his eyes penetrating to the core of my being. He placed his hand on my shoulder. "You have learned much. Spirit has a great task for you that is only beginning to unfold, and I was chosen to assist you in finding the pathway that will lead you to your task. Have patience. Much can be known and much can be done in the name of Spirit. I am only a guide whose vibration you have experienced. The vibration exists everywhere. Spirit will open your eyes and your heart to the truth you seek. I cannot provide an answer for my words would only distort your truth."

B . . . But Lou," I asked. "How can I know? How can I understand?"

"Look within. There you will find the answers. They have been there for eternity. Remember the things I have shown you. Look within."

He shoved me into Andres' car and slammed the door. Andres' responded immediately, releasing the brake and jerking the car into gear. As we bumped down the hill towards the road, I leaned out the window. Lou waved and put hands to his mouth, "Don't forget who you are. We are the same. We are Spirit."

He said something else, but the noise of Andres' car drowned out his voice. We rounded a curve and he disappeared from view.

I stared out the window into the mist that draped over the mountains. The clouds deadened my senses and my mind wandered aimlessly through a world of incredible visions.

I was pleased with the results of my trip, but the experience seemed unreal, incongruous with the world I'd accepted for so long. I knew the questions that had surfaced during the past few months wouldn't stop. Life would continually present questions with which I'd have difficulty. But I'd received a great gift and hoped to find it easier to deal with a shortage of answers.

Andres' maintained a tight grip on the steering wheel, looked straight ahead, and made no attempt at conversation. I doubt he could have spoken with me anyway. His knowledge of English appeared to be severely limited. And I enjoyed the silence; I needed it. I hoped he had understood Lou's instructions.

As we drove along, the steep, rugged terrain gave way to rolling hills, then to a fertile flood plain. We were forced to take a longer, more circuitous route to avoid the area where I experienced the mudslide, and I enjoyed the variations in scenery. However, much of the beauty of the passing landscape was lost on a mind somewhat out of focus, and I spent my time thinking about how to incorporate the things I'd seen into my reality.

Once we arrived at the airport, I hurried to the ticket counter, apprehensive about the prospects for catching a flight home. The ticket I held was for the following Friday—I'd had no idea how to schedule my trip—and I was concerned about the availability of a flight. I didn't relish the thought of spending a day or two in the airport, and was pleased when the agent informed me that a flight with an available seat would be leaving in three hours. Maybe Lou was still helping.

As I boarded the plane, I looked back towards Manila. The Philippines had opened doors for me in ways I never dreamed possible. It seemed odd, yet strangely appropriate, that I would have found such incredible wisdom in a place lacking all the trappings I'd previously associated with advancement.

I'd spent most of my adult life cluttering my mind with useless trivia and had been blinded to the truth of my existence. I was thankful Lou had allowed me to share in the understanding that seemed so common in his wonderful country.

The long flight home provided an opportunity to reflect upon Lou's teachings. I pondered what he had described as the three keys to knowledge:

ILLUSION. It's easy to see how we lose ourselves in the illusion of life. I think we're supposed to. That seems to be how it works. Becoming attached to the illusion is the problem.

When I stop to think about it, to analyze it, I realize that one dream can be no more valid than another. My finite and distorted view of the world does not allow me to fully comprehend the true nature of my experiences, cannot allow me to commune with infinite reality; but as long as I remember I'm dreaming, I can both enjoy and learn from my dreams.

ONENESS. What a wonderful concept. All things are connected. When I observe without emotion, I can see it. Nothing else makes sense.

Experiencing the connection leads to a respect for all life, and once experienced, it's impossible to continue the immoral and destructive practices we have inflicted upon both our planet and our fellow travelers in our spiritual evolution.

LOVE. What we often think of as the easiest concept to understand, to accept, may be the most difficult. We lack a true understanding of love.

Our marriages, families, friendships, and the condition of our world all demonstrate our unwillingness to give love totally and unselfishly. Love that emanates from Spirit is pure and complete, opens us to new levels of consciousness, released from the bonds of ego-centered thought.

When we become aware of our spiritual nature and allow our lives to be expressions of love, everything else falls into place, and conversely, when we understand the concept of illusion and acknowledge our Oneness, the love is already there.

Intellectually, I grasped the three concepts. I wondered how well I would integrate them into my life. Could I change my direction, my thinking, from the mundane to the spiritual? Throughout the remainder of the flight, I thought about all that had occurred and repeatedly played a moving picture of my experiences in the Philippines.

I was exhausted, wandering through a dream world that seemed a continuation of my mind-expanding journey. I needed rest in order to maintain my sanity. I even considered the possibility I'd gone mad and had conjured up the fantastic events that were imprinted on my memory. And I knew there was no one I could recount my story to—none to believe me if I did.

Several days passed before I returned my attention to completing the book. I'd been home almost a week before calling Mike. I'd needed time to myself and was reluctant to deal with his questions about the journey.

The trip had exacted a toll, both mentally and physically. I'd lost weight—fifteen pounds in two weeks—but my mind seemed heavy, filled with troubling thoughts. Though I tried to put the experiences into perspective, I couldn't think clearly, wondering about the changes taking place in my life. My thoughts were a confusing array of emotion: elation over my new awareness, depression as I wondered where it would lead.

The perfect place to reflect was down in Wareham on *Conquest*. The boat was an ideal environment in which to regain my strength. For me the sea holds an ability to purify and rejuvenate far beyond the capacity of its minerals. Coming home was like a reunion with a best friend, and once on board I slept for most of two days.

When I finally called Mike, I was concerned that he might be perturbed about my delaying the book. Not only was he not upset, he seemed almost giddy to hear from me.

"Dan," he said. "I'm so glad you're back. I can't wait to hear about your trip and to tell you what's happened while you were gone. I've just recruited a Chinese doctor who's trained in both Western and Oriental medicine. I've seen him in action, and it's better than I could have hoped for. Tell me about your trip. Did you see Lou?"

"It was good, really good," I said. How could I begin to describe the events I'd experienced?

"Did you see more healings? Did you get what you needed for the book?"

"Yeah," I said. "I'm working on it now. I'll have it in a few days."

"Great," Mike said. "I met a publisher while you were gone and showed him the rough draft. He wants to see it as soon as you're finished. I think he's really interested."

Mike talked about the book and how it would compliment the opening of his healing centers. It was good that he didn't ask for the details of my trip. I wasn't ready to discuss it. I wasn't certain I ever could.

Although Mike was more open to the subject than anyone I knew, his focus was upon the results of his work and less to the cause behind it. That was okay, I thought, the healing part was obviously important, and if he shared my inquisitive nature, it might delay his work.

****

With my strength returning, I worked late into the nights, oblivious to the world around me as I revised and polished the book. Sections that had previously frustrated me flowed without effort onto the page. It was as if the words came from somewhere outside of me.

192

My experiences with Eleuterio seemed to make the writing easier, made the concepts congeal into a more interesting form. It wasn't, of course, that I could include any of the strange events from my trip. Having experienced them though, tied everything together and allowed me to write with conviction and purpose, giving more credibility to the book.

I sat at the keyboard, typing page after page until my fingers ached, but refused to stop, fearing the spell might be broken. Although I slept and ate little, I seemed to gain energy as the book took form.

When I finally showed the book to Mike, he was elated. He stayed up all night, he said, reading and reviewing it. He seemed genuinely pleased.

"This is great stuff," he said, patting the book with his hand. "I want us to share equally in the credit—and the rewards. I'm taking it to the publisher on Monday."

"This book does everything I hoped it would, and more. You really made it flow. You were right about your trip making it better. It made a tremendous difference, and I liked it before you changed it."

"Thanks," I said. "You've been very generous all through the project. It's much more than I expected. I hope the book accomplishes everything you wished."

I reached out and shook his hand. "I'm going to miss working with you," I said. "It was great. You've been both patient and understanding and helped make the book what it is today. And, more importantly for me, the experience of writing the book has changed my life in ways you can't imagine. I'm deeply grateful for the opportunity you gave me. Thank you so much."

"No, thank you," Mike said. "I could never have completed this without your help. This book, this fantastic book, will really promote our healing work. The medical community can't ignore us now. They'll have to listen."

Mike was right. The book was released a few months later and immediately gained acceptance, which proved that the public was hungry for knowledge about alternative healing. Mike's impressive medical credentials caused us to get lots of notice in the press. Some controversy, however, was generated by powerful forces in traditional medicine that tried to squelch the rising tide of interest, but their objections stimulated even greater sales.

The publisher was understandably excited and made every effort to capitalize on the publicity. Mike and I spent several months doing interviews, book signings, and making the rounds of local radio and television talk shows. Though it was an exhausting schedule, it was one of the most exciting times I could remember.

In less than a year, we'd made the bestseller list and I was earning more money than I had in years. I began to receive other offers for book deals, but I wasn't ready to commit to anything new. I needed to spend time absorbing the marvelous experiences I'd had and determining what course to follow next.

My newfound wealth gave me the opportunity to overhaul Conquest and return her to sailing condition once again. I looked forward to taking her on some of the long trips that had previously been too dangerous. Returning to Bar Harbor would be nice. There were some wonderful little villages along the way where you could find the best seafood in the world.

Everything was moving fast. I was a writer, a legitimate and published writer, having accomplished what few writers ever attain. I was grateful to all those in my old life who had tolerated my indifference and my inflated ego and grateful to my new friends who had helped me regain my focus. Life had taken a new direction and, for a time, it seemed almost perfect.

The wealth and prestige were both great, and the money couldn't have come at a more appropriate time. Soon however, the allure began to wear off, leaving me with many of my old feelings of self-doubt. Was success with the book a fluke, and was it the culmination of my journey?

I felt stuck, trapped between two worlds. I was again experiencing a lifestyle of prominence and freedom, a lifestyle that held a powerful attraction. It was all too easy to fall into a meaningless routine of self-gratification.

Then, there was the other world, the one Lou had shown me. Once I'd seen it, I was unable to lose myself in a life of illusion; yet, I was unable to integrate myself into his world. I felt the second way offered the path I should follow, but I wasn't sure I could make such a drastic change. I searched for something, an awareness or feeling that would let me know I was on the right track, and I couldn't find it. I was stuck.

CHAPTER 15

AWAKENING

One evening, as I sat on deck, watching the play of moonlight on the water, I had what I considered to be a great idea. I would drive to Boston and do some research for a book concept I'd kicked around for several years. I'd once toyed with the idea of writing a novel, set in the eighteenth century, which dealt with the philosophical explorations of that period. During that time, a number of radical ideas were presented that became the basis of much of our thought today. With the time and financial resources to develop the concept, I felt it was worth a try.

While in Boston, I might give Kay a call. Though we hadn't spoken in more than a year, there had been many times I'd thought about our encounter in Ted's office. Since returning from the Philippines, however, my energy had been focused upon writing and promoting the book, and I'd refused to acknowledge any feelings I had for her. My life didn't seem sufficiently stabilized for any sort of relationship. Everything was so new, so different. I wanted to be certain the good things would last.

On the drive to Boston, however, I decided to call. I wanted to see Kay and share some of my experiences. I'd never yet told anyone about some of the more bizarre parts and wondered if she might be interested.

I was excited about my book idea. A new and different type of project might force me to forget the questions that clouded my thinking. Maybe I could finally enjoy life.

Spending time in Boston was great, and the research was fun. I get a sense of accomplishment in discovering facts and ideas others have overlooked or forgotten, and I always give myself a secret challenge to discover at least one unacknowledged bit of trivia.

However, it soon became evident that my idea might not be as simple as I'd hoped, and I called Jim Barton, the publisher who had produced our book. I wanted to see what he thought before I expended too much effort.

When Jim answered the phone, he seemed excited to hear from me. "Dan, I'm so glad you called. I've been trying to reach you for days. No one knew where your were. Didn't you get my messages? We, that is, you and Mike, have an opportunity to do a national TV talk show. It would be great for all of us. Millions would see it."

197

"No," I said. "I haven't been home in more than a week. I'm here in town. Just came up to do a little research."

"Boston? You're in Boston?"

"Yeah, I'm working on a concept for a book. I'd like to run it by you sometime, see what you think."

"Great. I'd love to have another book from you. Want to discuss it over dinner?"

"Sure. When would you like?"

"How about tonight?" he asked. "The wife's out of town and I'm tired of sandwiches. Where are you staying? I'll come by and pick you up."

"I'm in a little inn off Comm Ave, near the bridge."

"Yeah, I know the place," he said. "There's a great Chinese restaurant just a few blocks away. You in the mood for Chinese?"

"Sure. I've never met a won ton I didn't like," I joked.

"Then, I'll pick you up about seven if that's okay.

"That's fine. See you at seven."

I hung up the phone and decided to go for a walk. The area around my hotel, known as Back Bay by the locals, has some of the most spectacular architecture in the city. I spent the next few hours browsing the numerous shops and saw some of the most wonderful and expensive antiques I've ever seen. I don't know why I like the shops so much. I rarely buy anything. I suppose it's the connection with history that intrigues me. I enjoy rummaging through the past, sometimes wished I'd studied archeology or anthropology.

I returned to the hotel for a quick shower, excited about my opportunity to try my writing skills in a different genre. I dressed and walked down to the bar to wait for Jim.

"Double Chivas on the rocks," I called to the bartender.

He placed my drink on the counter, and I paused, gazing into the glass. Thoughts of the past year filled my mind. It seemed like a dream. I took a sip, then pushed the glass away. I didn't want it. Though I'd avoided alcohol since completing the book, fearing a return to my days of drinking too much, I'd never intended to quit altogether. But something had changed, and I sensed another part of my past drifting away. I paid for the drink and slid off the stool.

Jim stepped into the lobby as I emerged from the bar. After a quick greeting, he drove us to the restaurant where I outlined my idea over dinner. He listened politely, without comment.

"What do you think?" I asked.

"It's an interesting idea," he said. "But I'd hate to see you waste your talent and efforts on something that would have such a limited appeal. You'd have a small audience among the more sophisticated, intellectual types, but our research has shown that market is hardly worth the effort. Such books rarely recoup their production costs."

"I appreciate your opinion," I said. "You're the expert. I don't want to spend the next year working on a project that's going to bomb. Probably wouldn't do much toward enhancing my reputation either."

"Sorry," he said. "I get the feeling it's something you really want to do, but you should re-think it a bit. Perhaps you can put a different twist on it and come up with an angle that would work."

"Don't be sorry," I said. "It was only an idea. I'll try something else."

We made small talk for a time, and I agreed to do the TV show Jim had mentioned earlier. Finally, I told him I needed to go.

"I plan to return to Wareham tomorrow," I said. "Better go back to the hotel and get my things together."

Jim paid the check and we stepped outside. A crisp breeze was blowing off the bay. "I think I'll walk," I said. "It's a beautiful night and the fresh air will do me good."

The truth was, I was disappointed my idea had failed to stimulate Jim, but I was pragmatic enough to respect his opinion. He was the expert, and I wasn't prepared to cope with failure of any description.

As I walked through the streets of Back Bay, I thought about the way the area had grown. Once, nothing more than marshland, the area had been filled in during the eighteen-fifties, to allow for Boston's growth. Commonwealth Avenue, known by the natives as, "Comm Ave," is the centerpiece of the project. Fashioned after the *Champs 'Elysees*, it's lined with many of the area's historic buildings and offers some of Boston's most interesting sights.

I lost track of time as I walked along, imagining how the area must have appeared a century earlier. I wished I could take a trip into the past to see it as it once was. Detached from the present, I ambled along, oblivious to the distance I was covering.

Finally, aware that I'd gone more than a mile, I stopped and turned towards my hotel, but the prospect of walking back had little appeal. I looked for a taxi, but at that hour and in that area, finding one was unlikely. I began walking.

I'd gone only a couple of blocks when a taxi sped by and turned down the street ahead. It sounded as if it had stopped. I ran to the corner to see if I could catch it. The taxi was parked on the opposite side of the street, and someone was getting out. "Taxi. Taxi." I called. I ran towards the open door.

The passenger paid his fare and closed the door. The driver gave no indication he'd heard me.

"Taxi!" I yelled.

As I reached the door, the driver put the car in gear. I banged my fist against the side and yelled once more, but the driver continued to ignore me. He pulled slowly away, and I ran alongside, yelling.

The driver never acknowledged my calls, and the car picked up speed. As I abandoned my chase, assuming he didn't want another fare, the driver looked into his rearview mirror. For a brief moment we made eye contact.

Those eyes! Those dark, piercing eyes I would never forget. It was Lou!

The car sped away. I'd only seen him for a couple of seconds, but there was no doubt. It was Lou. I've never been more certain of anything in my life. But why? How?

My heart raced as I questioned the experience. I looked around to locate the taxi's passenger. Maybe he could provide some clue to what had happened, but the street was deserted. There was no indication where he'd gone.

I paused to catch my breath and sat down on the edge of one the planters lining the street. It was insane. It couldn't have happened, but my mind said that it had. Regardless of how bizarre the experience seemed, I knew I'd seen Lou.

Why hadn't he stopped? He knew it was me. His appearance had been no accident. But what purpose did it serve? None that I could imagine. Except to get me into a state of complete confusion.

I looked around, hoping to see a phone. Maybe I could call a cab. The street was deserted and there was no phone in sight. I took a few steps and paused at the entrance to an antique shop, closed for the night. An old man was huddled in the shadows, his head leaning against his knees.

"Excuse me," I said. "Do you know if there is a phone around here. I need to call a taxi."

The old man never raised his head but pointed to his left. "Around the corner," he whispered. His voice was low and raspy. "You will find what you need at the hospital."

"Thanks." I reached into my pocket and tossed him five dollars. "Good luck," I said.

I walked to the corner and looked ahead. A couple of blocks away, bright lights illuminated a large gray building. The sign out front read, "All Saints Children's Hospital."

I took a few steps as the old man called to me. "Why do you always think I want money from you?"

I ran back to the corner, wondering if . . . No, it couldn't have been. I looked at the doorway where the old man had been sitting. He was gone. I leaned against the building to catch my breath, then turned toward the hospital. I was in no shape to walk to the hotel.

The street was a blur. My mind was unable to grasp what had happened. Strange thoughts came and went without conscious effort on my part.

When I reached the hospital, my heart was pounding, and I walked up the steps to the entrance. Across the lobby a lady was seated behind a large circular desk. I asked her to direct me to a pay phone. "That way," she said, pointing across the hall. "Next to the vending machines."

A row of chairs lined the wall near the entrance, and I walked over to await my cab. I was in shock and stared ahead, watching the reflections of the lights and movements in the glass before me.

I'd been seated for several minutes when I heard the sound of the double doors at the end of the hall. I turned to see the figure of a woman step through the doors and into the corridor. In my stupor I found it difficult to focus on her as she began walking toward the exit near where I was seated. Something seemed out of place. I couldn't determine what was wrong, but I felt she didn't belong.

As the woman approached, her face registered in my mind and our eyes met. It was Kay!

"Dan," she gasped. "What are you doing here?"

"What are you doing here?" I asked.

"I volunteer, a couple of nights a week. I've done it for several years, but what brings you here? Someone ill?"

"No," I said. "I came in to use the phone. Need a cab."

"What do you do?" I asked. "It's not exactly the same as working at AFR."

"I read to the children, try to help them forget their illness, make them a little more comfortable. I was just leaving. I'm not usually here this late, but there's a little girl. She's very sick and needs a lot of attention. Can I give you a ride?"

"I called a cab, but yeah, I'd like that. Could we stop and get a cup of coffee?"

"Sure," she said. "That would be nice. What about your taxi?"

As Kay asked, the cab pulled up in front of the building.

"I'll take care of him," I said.

I walked over and handed the driver a twenty. "Changed my mind," I said. He took the money, and as he pulled away, I could see him shaking his head.

Kay drove us to an all-night diner, and we went inside, taking a booth at the far end. When the waitress approached, I said, "Couple of coffees please."

"I'll have a cup of tea," Kay corrected.

"Make it two teas," I said.

"How have you been?" I asked. "I know you'll find this hard to believe, but I was planning to call you, or at least, I wanted to. I think about you a lot, but I wasn't sure if you wanted to hear from me. I mean, I know I've been pretty inconsiderate. I guess I wondered what you really thought about me."

Kay looked at me and smiled. "I know," she said. "You don't have to explain."

I felt she understood. We sat for several minutes, silently staring into each other's eyes, communicating with a clarity and eloquence that isn't possible with words. There seemed to be a connection with her that had never been broken.

Seeing her in such a miraculous fashion had rekindled emotions that had been long dormant. I didn't want to let her slip away again. She was so confident, certain of her place in the universe. I wondered if I could be a part of her life.

As I looked into her eyes, I reflected upon the extraordinary coincidence that had brought us together again. It had to be more than a chance occurrence. Could it be another door Lou was opening for me?

"How did you come to be involved with volunteer work?" I tried to re-focus my attention. "I'll have to say it surprises me," I said.

"I began soon after you left the company," she said. "A friend of mine was working at the hospital and asked me to help out while she was on vacation. A week later, I was hooked. The children are so appreciative and seem so helpless. I couldn't resist.

"Believe it or not," she said. "I was going to call you. I read your book. I love it. It plants the seeds of hope for thousands of people who've been abandoned by traditional medicine.

"I thought there might be some way you could help with the children. Maybe you could convince Dr. West to invest some of his time with them."

Kay melted me with her sense of caring. Her devotion to the children was obvious, and I was impressed by her dedication to her work.

"I might be able to do something," I said. "There were many things I couldn't include in the book, phenomena most people wouldn't believe. I saw healings, miraculous and instantaneous healings that I can't begin to describe.

"With your interest in healing you would have marveled at the things I saw. I hope you don't think I sound crazy."

"Not at all," she said. Her eyes were sparkling. "I'd love to hear more. I've been taking some classes in an ancient Chinese practice called, Qi-Gong. The instructor is teaching us how we can manipulate a person's energy field and help them overcome disease. I sometimes use it on the children as I sit with them. I do it discreetly, of course. I don't think the hospital would approve."

"You know about Qi?" I said. I was shocked. "Many of the healings I've seen are the result of the manipulation of Qi or Prana, as some call it.

"But healing the body is just the beginning," I said. "I've only begun to reach a point where I can accept some of what I've seen." I paused and thought about seeing Lou and the old man. "There's still a lot I don't understand."

During the next two hours we talked about the recent past and the way our lives had changed. I told Kay as much as I dared about my experiences in the Philippines, leaving out the more bizarre parts, and she seemed interested.

I saw a side of her I'd never before experienced. Kay had a depth of spirit, of compassion, I'd never known and shared so many of my thoughts and concerns, it was uncanny.

"I'm afraid I've been doing most of the talking," I said. "Once I get started, it's hard to stop me. I hope I'm not boring you."

"On the contrary," she answered. I could listen all night, but it's pretty late, and I still have to go to work tomorrow—or I guess it's today." She looked at her watch. "I need to go."

I paid the check and we walked to her car. As I opened her door, she said, "I'd love to see you again. There seems to be so much we have in common. And I was serious about helping with the children. You'd love it."

When we arrived at my hotel, Kay held my hand. "Let's get together again," she said. "I hope you'll consider what I asked. I think we can do something meaningful."

"I'll call you." I said. I stepped onto the curb and leaned in the window.

"Promise?" she said. "I'd like to hear about the other things too."

"Yes. I'm going back to Wareham tomorrow, but I'll call you when I get home. We can talk about your idea. I promise."

We said goodbye and I watched her drive away. What an unusual night, I thought. But then, everything that had happened since my journey began seemed strange. I wondered where it was leading.

Once in my room I thought about all the extraordinary coincidences that had occurred, all the events that had culminated in meeting Kay. What did it mean? And where did Lou fit in?

I walked to the door that led to the balcony and stepped out. A light mist had formed, bathing the river in an eerie glow. In the distance the crescent moon glistened on the water, and I recalled a similar scene from the past, a time devoid of vision and purpose, when I'd once considered, "checking out" on life. I could see that death had been the correct choice, but not death in the physical sense. What I had needed, what I experienced, was not a death of the flesh, but the death of my old and misguided ego and a rebirth into the world of Spirit. New and exciting possibilities were opening before me, in a world I'd previously ignored, and I was grateful for being given an opportunity to experience it.

I was excited about calling Kay, and would try to get Mike interested in working with the children. Perhaps I could help them too. Maybe I could talk Lou into coming and sharing some of his knowledge.

Lou. How could I have survived without his help. Regardless of how little emphasis he placed upon teachers, his guidance and wisdom had probably saved my life. I thought about the three concepts he had given me.

ILLUSION. ONENESS. LOVE. The simplicity was obvious, and yet, the implications were more powerful and offered more potential for positive change than anything I'd ever experienced. My challenge would be to integrate those principles into my life, living and experiencing without limitation.

How would I accomplish such a task? I understood the futility of rationalization and the need to release, allowing my destiny to unfold without judgment. But how would I know if I'd chosen the right path?

It was obvious why Lou had never given me the answer. There wasn't one. Though he told me so on many occasions, I never fully grasped what he meant. Finally, I understood.

Suddenly, everything made sense—Lou's teachings, my experiences—everything blended into enlightenment. Though my path had seemed difficult, it was no worse or no better than any other. All paths ultimately lead to understanding. That explained why the books I'd read and the teachings I'd pursued had failed to create the state of awareness I sought. I had searched for ultimate truth as if it were a tangible object.

My experiences with Lou wouldn't make my life easier. Because of my new level of understanding, life might become more difficult than ever.

I saw how my understanding, my enlightenment, would never remove what I'd mistakenly perceived to be the pain and misery of life, but would only help me accept those impostors with the understanding that a higher purpose was at work. I would sometimes still experience confusion, sometimes feel pain. Outwardly, life might appear much as it had in the past.

Would that be an improvement? Had I progressed from my old self? In many ways I'd never changed at all. I was very much a part of the world, very much involved in the mundane actions and conflicts of a confused and tumultuous life. The difference for me was that I'd developed a degree of understanding and had experienced a dramatic shift in my perception and awareness.

For years I'd attempted to change my circumstances in order to find happiness. Finally, I could see that the only thing needing change was my perception, my attitude towards my circumstances.

I don't know why things happen as they do and perhaps never will, but I can see how my experiences are necessary for my spiritual evolution, my advancement toward Oneness. It's all part of a unique process. Will I ever feel doubt again? Probably. Will I ever question my purpose, my path? Certainly. But my questions and doubts are diminished when viewed through an awareness of self.

Looking back over my searching, I'm amused by the seriousness with which I've tried to rationalize the unseen world. I've sought enlightenment as if my life depended upon it, and in a way it did, but there was never a time limit to my search. It didn't matter. In a larger sense, the things that have played such important roles in my life, including my searching, are totally unimportant. I've found no path worthy of pursuit except the pursuit of Oneness, and yet, I can see how even that goal is not to become my obsession. I've learned how to be, to release, and thus experience my true self in which is found all the things I've sought for so many painful years.

What happens next? How will my experiences with Lou impact my future. I can't imagine. Yet, I look ahead with excitement, for I know I'll encounter challenges and will grow in ways I've never dreamed possible. I only hope I can become more sensitive to the sometimes subtle opportunities I've overlooked in the past. I've seen incredible realities, events far beyond my comprehension, and briefly touched other dimensions. And one question still remains. Why me?

I might have stumbled across my path without Lou's help, but he had made it more visible. Lou was the catalyst for an astounding transformation, a metamorphosis that liberated me from the bondage of ego. Through him I'd discovered a fascinating new world where dreams and reality converge.

Had I really seen Lou? I wasn't sure. Had he somehow materialized himself into my world, or was the experience merely a vision he implanted in my mind? The answer made no difference, for there was no distinction between those two alternatives. Both are parts of the dream. The significance is that something created a profound change within me, a change in the way I perceive the universe. I was certain Lou had been a part of it. Without his guidance I don't know what turns I might have made. He taught me that there are reasons for everything, that we find meaning and purpose when we open ourselves. The meaning is always there. When we listen, we find it. And I had only begun to listen. I catch brief glimpses of the beauty, the majesty of life with all its entanglements, and I love it dearly.

The questions I'd suffered upon myself for so many years no longer caused pain. Within each I'd found the seeds for more than one correct answer, and my senses detected an infinite number of questions yet to be asked.

I closed my eyes and heard Lou's voice. "You have arrived at the point of your beginning, your awakening to true self. Your journey, your lessons, have only begun. Prepare for the lessons to come. Share your knowledge and it will continue to grow and enrich you.

"Remember the three keys and know that you are responsible for your life. Only you can choose between pain and happiness, can choose to accept the love that fills the universe. Never doubt that life is unfolding with the perfection which is Spirit. The perfection you seek to understand."

Whatever would come, I knew I was more prepared than ever before. I felt a warm surge of energy and opened my eyes to the heavens. Above the horizon the moon was swathed in a blanket of stars, a scene more beautiful than ever. I stared beyond the moon, beyond the universe, into the intense blackness of space. Infinity.

On the screen in my mind words appeared:

I am a butterfly,
a molecule of air.
I am a star,
a blade of grass;
I am everywhere.
I am the waters of the sea,
the wind across a plain,
a phosphorous moon on autumn night,
a single drop of rain.

I roam the forests, unexplored,
ascend to snow-topped peak.
I drift in gossamer mists, aloft
and journey distant streets.
I see through eyes of everyman
and know his secret thought.
Each day I create and destroy,
the wonders I have wrought.

Omniscient and all-powerful, and yet,
I fail to see
the truth that lifts me
from this guile,
that God is all,
is me.

The End

Some of this book was based upon my experiences with the Shuar, an indigenous people of the Ecuadorian rain forest. My time with them was made possible through the efforts of my friend, John Perkins and his organization, Dream Change Coalition.

Those interested in participating in rain forest preservation or in learning more about the peoples of the Amazon can contact DCC at:

Dream Change
P.O. Box 31357
Palm Beach Gardens, FL 33420
or
www.dreamchange.org